Dirty Rich Cinderella Story

EVER AFTER

D1518754

NEW YORK TIMES BESTSELLING AUTHOR

LISA RENEE JONES

ISBN-13: 9781726804837

DEAR READERS:

Dirty Rich Cinderella Story: Ever After is Cole and Lori's second book. This is what happens on their honeymoon, and after! If you haven't read their first book: Dirty Rich Cinderella Story, please be sure to read it first as that is where Cole and Lori's story begins.

Thank you so much for picking up your copy, and I hope you enjoy where Cole and Lori are about to take you!!

Xoxo,
Lisa Renee Jones

CHAPTER ONE

Lori

Honeymoon in Paris

On our final day after a week in Paris for our honeymoon, Cole decides he wants to get us arrested. Not literally, but his actions say that's exactly what he wants to do. After a day spent sightseeing, we dress up for an evening out with plans to visit our favorite little bakery for dessert and coffee. I wear a sexy red dress in a clingy material, with deeper cleavage than usual and a zipper that parts the dress top to bottom in the front. It's a daring dress when I am not usually all that daring, but this is Paris and I'm with my *husband*. Cole personifies tall, dark and gorgeous in a blue button-down with dress slacks, and the way his eyes light on me as if he wants to gobble me up has heat rushing through my body.

We enter the elevator of our hotel, and the minute the doors close, he pulls me to him. "You're beautiful, wife," he murmurs, his voice all rough-edged and sexy.

My hand flattens on his chest, his heart thundering under my palm. "You're not so bad yourself, husband."

I've barely spoken the words before his hand is at the back of my head and he's crazy, hot, kissing me, his hands caressing a path up my back. I moan with the lick of his tongue, telling myself to stop this. We're in a public place, but then his tongue is stroking mine again and I am lost, sinking into the hard lines of his body, only remotely aware of the ding of the elevator.

Cole presses me into the corner of the car, and pulls his lips from my lips, his eyes burning into mine a moment before voices sound just behind him. A rush of people swarm the car and Cole settles against the wall, pulling my back to his front, the hard ridge of his erection nestling my backside. I am aroused, wet, aching all over for this man, and ready to go back upstairs. My hand closes down on his hand where it settles on my belly and the rest of the ride down is eternal until finally the car halts. Cole leans down and whispers in my ear, "I'm going to obsess over that zipper all night long."

My lips curve, a shiver racing down my spine as he nips my lobe. *Yes. Please. Think about it.* I love the Cole that wants and wants and wants more. That was the idea when I slipped into this dress. I am about to voice just that, but already he's lacing his fingers with mine, leading me out of the car, and it's only a few moments before we're on the street, headed toward our dinner destination.

A short walk from our hotel on Champs-Élysées, Ladurée is a cozy spot world-renowned for their macarons, which has caused me about a five-pound gain on this trip. They also serve dinner, and once we're inside the bakery, we approach the hostess. Soon we are turning to the rooms on our right and headed up a staircase where we are seated at a tiny corner table. Everything is tiny in Paris, and while Cole's leg is intimately pressed to mine, he's forced to behave since I could practically lean and I'll be touching the man next to me.

Cole places our dinner orders for us with perfect, sexy French, a language that he apparently excelled at during school. I *approve*. Once the waitress leaves us alone again, we chat about our week and even our eventual caseload when we return home. I love that we are this connected. That we share so very much. I've never experienced this in my life, with anyone. Time flies by with us laughing, flirting and enjoying good food, as well as sweet, bubbly champagne. We've just finished off our dessert and coffee when Cole leans forward. "Look, sweetheart. Since we're going home tomorrow, I need to fill you in on something."

My eyes go wide. "What something and why do I not know already?"

"Because I wasn't going to let you worry all week and before you panic, your mother is fine. I know that despite her recovery from her stroke, you worry, but it's not about her. That said, you know that large trials can come with protestors, and you're a protestor virgin no more. When you win a case, after the public prosecutes a client, like they did ours before we left for Paris, all hell breaks loose. We've had protestors at the office since we left, and that comes with random threats."

Again, my eyes go wide. "Threats?"

His hands slide over mine where it rests on the table. "It happens. If I could keep you away from this stuff, I would, but it's part of the job. And honestly, I didn't think our win was one of those trigger cases. It was televised. It was pretty obvious that our client was innocent."

"Will they target my mother?"

"Doubtful, but to be safe, I offered her and her new man a trip to the Hamptons to get out of the city for a while."

"And my mother refused," I assume, reaching for my purse to retrieve my phone.

"Easy, sweetheart," he says, catching my hand again. "I convinced her to go. All is well and the only reason I'm telling you now, not in the morning, is that I knew you'd want to talk to her before we leave. With the time zone difference, that means tonight."

Tension rolls across my chest and down my spine. "Right. Okay."

He narrows his eyes at me. "What are you thinking?"

That I'm worried, I think but I say, "That I need to go to the bathroom." I set my napkin down and stand up, barely avoiding the guy next to me as I hurry past our table and cut right toward a bathroom. I step inside the rather large room with no mirrors, two sinks, and four floor-to-ceiling doors, sealed shut. I've barely closed myself inside when Cole is joining me.

"What are you doing?" I demand, and already his big hands are on my waist, and he is pressing me against the wall.

"The bubble is not going to pop," he says. "Nothing bad is happening. This is normal."

"I know," I whisper, unsure how he's just put what I feel into words when I haven't even formed it into coherent thoughts until this moment.

"You don't know. You felt safe and then the rug was pulled out from under you when your father died. I'm not going to let that happen. You have me now. I'm not going anywhere. I promise."

"You can't promise that."

"I can," he says, his voice deep, rich, his tone absolute. "I will."

"People die."

"Yes, but if I die, you'll know how much I loved you. You'll know I'm still with you." He cups my face. "But you don't get to get rid of me that easily. Whatever waits for us here, there, or anywhere, we'll get through it together. That's what husbands and wives do."

Warmth and calm wash over me. "Husband," I whisper.

"Wife," he replies, his gaze raking over my lips, and lifting. "About that zipper."

"Take me to our hotel and I'll show you how it works."

"I can't wait that long," he counters, reaching for said zipper.

I catch his hand. "Cole," I warn urgently. "You have to wait."

I've barely finished that reprimand before his mouth is crashing down on mine and he's kissing me, his tongue stroking my tongue. One of his hands settles at the base of my spine, molding me close, all those hard, sinewy parts of him pressed to all the soft parts of me and I moan. Another second later, and my zipper is open, and he's pressed my hands over my head, his fingers dragging over the thin lace of my barely-there bra, teasing my nipples.

"We can't do this here," I whisper, and I mean it, despite the moan that rolls from my throat, as his fingers slide between my legs, heat pooling low in my belly and spreading to the touch of his fingers.

"And yet we are," he says.

Voices sound just outside the door, and I panic. "Cole," I hiss.

He reacts, and in an instant, his arm is around my waist and he's pulling me into a long, narrow stall, shutting the heavy door and locking it. Women, two I think, enter the bathroom, and Cole steps back in front of me, his cheek pressing to mine as he whispers. "I'm going to make you come with them standing right there."

My fingers curl on his chest. "No," I silently whisper, but he swallows the protest with a deep lick of his tongue, and just like that, he's grabbed my panties and yanked them away.

And then he's kneeling on one knee, his lips pressing to my belly, and the effect is an adrenaline rush up and down my body. My fingers tangle in his hair and I tell myself it's to pull him away, but his tongue flicks my belly button and

I bite my lip to silence my pleasure. I know where that tongue is headed and it's almost too much.

I manage to tug his hair after all, but it only seems to challenge him. He lifts my leg to his shoulder, his mouth closing down on me, and sensations spiral through me. I cave to the pleasure, my head falling back on the wall.

Then he is licking and exploring, merciless in his attention, his thumb stroking my clit, tongue delving in and out of my sex—around and around and everywhere. And when it's too much, just too much for this place, his fingers stretch me, pressing inside me, and I'm arching into him.

My pulse thunders in my ears, and the women just keep talking. They won't stop, but neither will Cole, but then again, I don't want him to stop. Every spot he touches and licks is bliss, and I'm right there on the edge of that mountaintop, so very close to tumbling over.

A ball of tension forms low in my belly and spreads, and then I'm there, my belly and sex clenching, and remotely I hear my breathing, a soft moan I cannot control escaping my throat. Pleasure overtakes me, stealing time, and then I go limp.

Cole eases my leg down, re-connecting my zipper, and sliding it up my body until it's back in place, and he's standing in front of me, kissing me, the taste of champagne and me on his lips before he whispers, "That was so damn hot."

My eyes go wide at the idea that the women can hear us. "They left," he promises. "Let's go back to the room and fuck. Then we'll call your mother and fuck again. Then we'll pack and fuck again. And finally, we'll go home. Because, sweetheart, as much as I love fucking you in Paris, I want you in my bed, which is now our bed."

The aftermath of my orgasm mixed with all the male perfection of this man, who is my husband, and best friend, fills me. It's then that it hits me that as perfect a Cinderella story our wedding and Paris honeymoon were, the real fairy tale is knowing that he's no fair-weather Prince. It's knowing that in an imperfect world, Cole can still make everything perfect. That I am not alone, and never will be again.

"I love you, Cole."

He strokes my cheek. "I love you too, sweetheart." And with that, he leads me out of the bathroom, past several gaping women, and right back to our table, where we eat more chocolate, pay the bill, and leave. *Together.* The way we will face whatever waits on us in New York City, now and always.

CHAPTER TWO

Cole

Every time I think that I have never wanted to be inside Lori more, I want more—sooner, faster, harder—just *more*. And with her by my side, walking toward our Paris hotel room, the taste of her on my lips, I can say I have never wanted to be inside her more than right this moment. And it's not just about sex or how much I fucking love this woman. It's about how much I want to wash away her fears; ease her need for control, because that control is rooted in tragedy; in her father's death and her mother's stroke. Not that I don't get the need for control, not that I want to take hers away. It's the reason she needs it that I want to tear away; her fears and her past that have cut deeply, perhaps more so than she realizes. But I realize. I see what she does not. Every moment to Lori is the moment before someone pulls the rug out from under her and us. Every moment is the moment she dared to just be happy when she believes she should have been thinking about how to protect her mother, or me, or us or everyone around her. So, yeah. I want to be inside her. I want to be next to her. I want and want and want, because then she has no room to do anything but feel, moan, and want right along with me. That's her sanity. That's our sanity. It's the place we can go to escape her fears until I drive them all away. And I will. Nothing that awaits us in New York City is unusual, but with her mother there and us here, the next twenty-four hours will be hell for her.

A crazy possessive need that I can't even explain—she's my damn wife, it's not supposed to get much more possessive—overcomes me and I wrap my arm around her shoulders and pull her closer, our legs and hips aligned. No one is taking her from me. A silly protest is not taking her from me. *Fuck*. What the hell is wrong with me?

I guide us across the street and to the hotel and a doorman opens the door for us. I actually have to force myself to let her go to allow her to enter the building first, but I'm right there, just behind her, quickly settling my arm back around her shoulders. She tilts that delicate chin up and gives me a soft, aroused look that tells me she feels the energy I'm radiating. I lean down and kiss her, keeping us in motion. The sooner we're in the room, the better. The sooner I'm fucking her, and loving her—I can't do the previous without the latter anymore—the better.

I manage to keep our pace quick but steady, and we're now at the elevator. I punch the button, but I don't look at Lori. If she tilts her mouth to mine again, I'm going to forget what a private person I am and devour her right here and now. For a high-end hotel, the doors open with such creeping slow-ass speed that I want to shove them open. I drag Lori into the elevator and against my body, all her soft perfect curves pressed to mine and she punches in our floor.

She tilts her chin, offering me her mouth, and I quickly turn her to face forward, resting her cute little backside against me, and holy hell, she's now nuzzled up against the ridge of my pulsing erection. Holy hell again. I think that pretty little backside needs a spanking. Her punishment for driving me this crazy without even trying. No woman should have that kind of control over a man, even his wife, and yet, I fucking love it. The floors tick by and I lean in, inhaling that sweet floral scent of her. "No woman should leave Paris without being spanked."

She sucks in a breath and tries to turn in my arms, but I catch her waist, a low laugh escaping my throat. There it is. The way to take her mind off the protestors and her mother. One of the few things that I haven't done since that first night we met. "Cole," she whispers, her hands going to mine, and my name is a rasp of desperation that is both need and panic.

"Don't worry, sweetheart," I murmur, nipping her earlobe. "I'll make it hurt so good."

She pants out a breath as if my mouth and hands are already all the places we both know they will be. The elevator dings and I push off the wall, my body cradling hers as I walk her forward, placing her between me and the yet-to-part doors. Adrenaline radiates off her, into me, and I can almost feel the pulse of her heartbeat as she wills the doors to open. Slowly, they creep left and right until they are wide enough for her to try to step forward, but I don't let her. I make her wait. I make me wait.

Only when the doors are fully open do I find her ear again and say, "Are you thinking about my hand?"

"Cole, damn it," she hisses, and I release her, laughing as she darts forward, with nowhere to go but our room, but she does what I expect. In true control freak mode, she stops at the door and turns, leaning against it to watch my every slow step toward her, as if she's in control when she knows that, right now, she's not, and we both like it that way. Later, she'll kick my ass if I act like a barbarian, but right now is not later.

I stop in front of her, but I don't touch her. "Ready to go inside, Mrs. Brooks?"

"Not without some rules."

My lips twitch. "What rules would those be?"

"If you spank me—"

"I'm *going* to spank you, Lori."

"If I say you can."

"Okay. Am I going to spank you, Lori?"

"I haven't decided." In that grab for control, she gives me her back and swipes her keycard to open the door My hand comes down on the handle, my body framing hers, my knee in front of her leg, blocking her entry. "Once we go inside, your pretty little ass is mine, unless you say no now."

She rotates and faces me, her hand settling on my cheek, her soft fingers rasping over my newly formed stubble. "Except," she says, "I know you'll always let me say no, even if I wait until we're inside." There is such tenderness in her eyes and voice that she undoes me. "Which is why the answer is yes. You can spank me, Cole. Because I married you for ten million reasons that include trust."

If I wasn't so damn hard I was about to break before those words, I'd be so damn hard I was about to break now. I'm not sure where that puts me now, besides needing inside the room. I take the key from her and swipe the card again. She rotates, her beautiful backside brushing my cock, and the minute I push the door open, she's inside the room, but she doesn't get far. I'm a step behind her, my reach long enough to catch her hand and pull her back to me, and by the time the door is shut, she's against it and I'm in front of her, my legs caging hers.

"I married you for ten million reasons too," I assure her, reaching for her zipper and pulling it all the way down, while I go down on a knee in front of her just long enough to lick her clit and hear her gasp before I'm back on my feet, turning her toward the wall to pull away her dress and bra in one quick swipe, to leave her in only her thigh highs and heels.

"One of those reasons," I say, "is your perfect ass." I smack her cheek in a tease of what is to come, and on her yelp, I turn her to press her back against the door. "The other," I continue, "among the too many to count," I clarify, "are your stunning breasts." I reach up and tease her nipple.

She swallows hard. "You married me for my ass and my—"

"Stunning breasts," I say. "The whole package, sweetheart. You're the whole package for me and that makes me a damn lucky man. Don't move. Understand?"

"Yes, *Mr. Brooks.* I understand."

My lips quirk. "I really love these rare moments when you just do what I say. Too bad I can't get you to listen with your clothes on." I toe off my shoes.

She laughs. "I could say the same of you, only you don't even listen when you're naked."

I pull my shirt off and press my hands to the wall next to her, my gaze raking her naked body before I look at her and say, "Of course I do. When you say 'harder, faster, more' I don't ever deny you, now do I?"

"I don't suppose you do," she whispers, breathless. I really love this woman breathless. "Face the door and don't even think about turning around."

"Is this when you—"

"I'll warn you. Do it."

She turns and I don't immediately move. I let her wait. I make us both wait, the sound of her breathing and my breathing the only whispers in the room. Seconds tick by until she whimpers, "Cole, damn it, you're killing me."

I drag my finger over her shoulder, goosebumps lifting in its wake. "Don't turn," I warn before I step back and finish undressing, and the sight of her in her heels and thigh highs, her backside waiting on my hand has me ready to bend her over the bed, spank her, fuck her and start over. I reel myself back in, wanting to show her just how much of an escape we can be together. On some level, before we go back to the states, I need her to know this. A need that claws at me in ways I can't understand and I don't question.

This is about more than a spanking. This is about that need to possess her that defies reason and won't be ignored. We won't be sleeping this last night in Paris.

CHAPTER THREE

Cole

I walk toward Lori and go down on one knee again, my hands at her ankles. She tries to turn and I flatten one palm on her lower back. "Move before I tell you and I'll spank you without warning. I might not even fuck you after. And you'll still like it."

"You wouldn't," she gasps.

"Wouldn't I? Move and you'll find out that answer. Are we clear?"

"Crystal," she says, that defiance I love in her overtaking her voice. "Just remember—what goes around comes around. You're next. Maybe not tonight, but soon."

I remove my hand and step close, but not close enough to touch her again, my hands pressing to the wall just outside hers. "Then I guess I better make your punishment worth mine?" I reply, my lips near her ear, my throbbing cock so damn close to the sweet wet heat of her body.

"I guess you better," she dares to challenge.

I smack her backside, firm but not hard, and when she yelps, my lips quirk, and my cock twitches. Damn, I love this woman. I don't give her time to recover from the shock, returning to her ankles, once more and my teeth scraping her pretty little backside. She arches her back, and I run my hands up the front of her thighs, my lips pressing to her lower back. I shift to her side, my lips at her hip, one hand on her belly and one on her backside.

"What comes next, Lori?" I ask, my teeth now scraping her hip.

"Apparently you spank me," she whispers.

"No apparently about it." I rub her cheek and give it another gentle but present smack, the fingers of my other hand sliding into the wet heat of her body at the same moment that she yelps again. "That's not a spanking," I say. "You know that, right?"

"Yes," she pants out. "I'm aware, that you're taunting me."

I smack her backside again and slide my fingers deep along the seam of her body. She moans and arches into my hand. "Does that feel like a taunt?"

"Yes," she whispers. "Yes, it does."

"Not pleasure? Because if it doesn't feel good, I can stop."

"You're evil, Cole."

"And you like it." I nip her hip and lave the offended skin before I push to my feet, my hands caressing a path over the porcelain perfection of her back and belly, until one hand is between her shoulder blades, while the other gently teases her nipples. She arches into the touch, and the instant she reacts, I turn her to face me, pressed against the wall, my hands back on the surface by her head, but I ensure we do not touch anywhere despite the fact that I want to touch her everywhere. I want to feel her everywhere.

My gaze rakes over her perfect curves, a slow inspection that has my body humming with how much I want her. "You're so fucking beautiful," I murmur, my voice low, rough with everything she makes me feel and want. No woman has ever made me feel anything like this.

"And this makes you want to spank me?"

"I *am* going to spank you and I'm going to do it because we both like it. I do. So do you." I push off the wall and back up. "Go to the bed and get on your hands and knees."

Her beautiful eyes spark with shock. "What?"

"You heard me. Go to the bed—"

"I heard. You want me to—"

"Yes. *Now*. The sooner you do it, the sooner we can fuck, and make love."

"Fuck or make love?"

I grab her and pull her to me, cupping her head and kissing the hell out of her. "Both," I say. "We can do both. That's who we are now."

She smiles, and her hand settles on my jaw. "Yes. That is who we are and—"

"And what?" I press.

"I like it."

My heart warms with those words. My heart has warmed in ways I didn't think possible with Lori, and it does so *because* of Lori. "I want you to like it," I assure her, walking backward and turning her until she's standing in front of the bed, my hands on her shoulders, erection at her hip, as I lean in and whisper. "Now do as I say." I lean in and kiss her. "On your hands and knees."

She reaches down, strokes my cock and then goes down on her hands and knees, clearly reminding me that she can test my control. With anyone else, I would not like this at all, but they are not her. With her, with my wife, I fucking love this challenge. I go down on a knee beside her, my hand, running up her belly and teasing her nipples before one palm settles at her backside and the other settles between her shoulder blades. I rub her backside, deep caresses, her soft, raspy breathing filling the air. Over and over I warm her skin, readying her, my fingers sliding into her sex, stroking her until she's so damn wet, she can be no wetter, waiting for that moment that finally comes.

"Are you going to warn me?" she asks.

"This is your warning," I say, and then smack her backside hard and fast two times, and then I shift and enter her, driving deep. I pull back and spank her again, driving into her, pulling back. I spank her again. I drive in again.

"Cole," Lori cries out, pleasure and need etched in my name that leaves no room for me to ask where she's at right now, what she wants, but still, I roll to my side, pulling her back to my chest, cupping her breast. "How are you right now?" I ask, my lips at her ear, needing to know she's with me, in this, fully aroused. "Are you with me, Lori?"

"How can you not know that answer?" She reaches behind her, grabs my hip and presses against me. "Does that answer your question?"

I lean around her, kissing her, our bodies grinding together as I do, and it's just not enough. I thrust into her, and she pants and covers my hand on her breast. Her body arching into the next pump of my cock. And the next. And the next. We are wild, frenzied, and I need her closer. I pull out, and she's turning to face me even before I can do it for her. A moment later, her hip is at my hip, and I'm driving into her again, our lips colliding, tongues stroking, that extra edge of intimacy, shifting the energy, taking us from fucking to making love.

We go from wild, frenzied need, to a slow simmering burn as I stroke hair from her face. "Do you know how crazy you make me? How absolutely and insanely in lust and love I am with you?"

"Good thing since you just married me," she says, her hand settling on my face. "And good thing I feel the same and—" I kiss her and there are no more words. We rock together, sway together, touch and kiss, and slowly shudder into release. We ease into relaxation and I roll Lori to her back, leaning over her. "Tell me you liked that."

"You know I did or you wouldn't have kept going."

"First thing that comes to your mind. Don't think. Just answer. What were you thinking about when I was spanking you?"

"I wasn't," she says. "I was just in the moment."

"Good. When you feel like the world is spinning and about to fall from under your feet, you come to me, and we'll escape. We'll make it stop spinning."

"Are you saying the world is spinning? What is going on?"

"Nothing but what I've already told you about the trial chaos. And nothing that won't go on over and over, and in different ways."

"I know. I get that."

"But the hell you went through is fresh for you and you're about to call your mother, who you almost lost not that long ago. I just want you to know that as you call her, as we go back to the real world that I can't promise you that world will never spin. I can't even promise, that I won't need you to steady it for me sometimes. But know this: I'll do the same for you. I promise you that we will steady it together."

"I know that," she says. "I said 'I do,' remember?"

"You did and I'm going to remind you of that many times and ways tonight. Call your mother." I kiss her hand. "But don't put any clothes on." I kiss her and push off the bed, walking to the door to find my phone before returning to the bed to offer it to her. She sits up and shivers.

"I think I need a shirt." She gives me a coy look. "You can take it off me after."

"And I will," I promise, moving back to the door to grab my shirt, which I drape around her. She shoves her hands into the sleeves and I help her roll them up, listening as she chats with her mother, laughing with joy at several things her mother says. When finally the chat is over, Lori's smile fades as she hands me back the phone. "What was bad enough that you felt they needed to leave the city, Cole? What haven't you told me?"

Tension rolls down my spine. "They didn't need to leave the city," I say. "But I know you. You'll worry if your mother is in the line of fire. I wasn't going to let you worry like that." I stand up and pull on my pants.

She scoots to the end of the bed. "You just put your pants on when I asked that question," she says. "As if you're preparing for some sort of battle. And you did so right after you gave me the spinning world talk."

Fuck. This woman knows me. I go down on one knee in front of her, taking her hand in mine. "It's normal. The chaos after a trial this big is normal."

"And yet, your reaction doesn't feel normal."

Because you've been threatened, I think. I've never had my wife, and the woman I love, threatened. But this time. I have. This time there are threats against Lori that I am not about to tell her about in full detail until we're home, security is in place, and her mother is close by. And if Walker Security does their job, there will be nothing to tell when we get home.

CHAPTER FOUR

Lori

Cole is still on his knee in front of me, tension radiating off of him. I reach out and run my fingers over the stubble of his jaw. "Talk to me. We're supposed to share everything now, remember?"

"We do, Lori. I'm also supposed to be the person that makes you feel safe and protected."

"I didn't marry you to feel safe and protected, Cole."

"But it's a need you have and if you're denying that, I'll just claim it for you. That need is why you didn't trust me at first."

"Cole," I breathe out, this man delivering so many feelings in me so very easily. "God, I love you, husband, but I don't need you to make me feel safe and protected and yet you do. Because the thing about life is, that when you have someone you know will endure the bad with you and make it better, you do feel safe and protected. I do—"

He presses his lips to mine, his hand at the back of my head, and there is tenderness and passion in this kiss. There is love. There is just so much. When his lips part from mine, he strokes my hair behind my ear. "Just move a little closer to me if the ground feels like it's falling. Okay?"

"Yes, but I need to say something that I fear is at work here. My father is why I didn't trust you at first. He was my hero that was flawed. I'm still accepting that but I don't want you to think that I need you to be perfect. I'm afraid I've made you feel that way."

"No," he says. "I get it. I know the hell he left you to clean up." He kisses my hand. "Perhaps we're dealing with my demons now, not yours."

"What does that mean?"

"It means I have you now. I'm not going to let anyone take you from me."

Realization hits me, Cole was far more alone when we found each other than I was. His parents are gone. He has no siblings. And yet this man was all in with me from the beginning. I made him fight for us. He did. So very perfectly.

He pushes off his knee, and sits on the bed beside me and takes me down on the mattress, the two of us lying side by side, facing each other. "Here's what I'm going to say to you before we head home. I'm going to be a bulldog about protecting you. You'll call it controlling. You might even be right. We'll fight. And we will talk, and then fuck it out. Deal?"

My lips curve, tenderness filling me at just how honest he's been with me. "The best deal ever."

It's almost twenty-four hours later, near sunset, when our plane touches down in New York City but that sexy encounter with Cole that turned tormented has been lingering in my mind. Actually, I'm pretty sure the entire encounter was driven by torment. I even believe that spanking was driven by his need to escape, not mine, or maybe both of us needed the escape.

Cole has remained edgy, his mood darker than usual, despite him touching me often, despite gentleness and love in his eyes when he looks at me. He's still fretting and while I don't deny he's told me the truth about what awaits us here in the city, I think he's got a gut feeling gnawing at him. And the man has an incredible gut feeling or he wouldn't be the all-star attorney that he is. Which is exactly why the minute we're taxiing on the runway, I dial my mother. "How are things?" I ask, fearful that trouble in the form of protestors or who knows what else might have found her.

"Glorious," she says, a smile in her voice. "This place Cole rented for us is incredible. He really shouldn't have done this. He's too generous, honey."

My heart warms with the knowledge that Cole has gone all-out for my mother, though it's not surprising to me at all. "He is," I say, my eyes meeting Cole's, his warm with a mix of affection and curiosity.

He arches a brow that says, "I am what?" no words needed. Often, Cole communicates with me with no words needed and I love this about him and us.

I smile and cut my gaze, intentionally leaving him guessing. "I need to go, mom," I say, "but call if you need us."

"Us," she murmurs. "I love the way you are an us with that man."

"Me too, actually," I say, amazed that she has latched onto the same word that I have, and about how much my life, and hers, has changed in less than a year.

"Love you," she says.

"Love you, too."

We disconnect as the plane pulls into the hangar. "I am what?" Cole asks, taking my hand.

"Arrogant. Good looking. Impossibly stubborn." I smile. "Generous. Driven. *Everything*. She says the place you have her staying at is incredible."

"That would be our weekend home that your mother has now officially seen before you."

I blanch. "What? Weekend home?"

"That's right," he confirms. "A client hooked me up with the property when I was still in Houston. I rent it out for a hefty fee, but now we can claim it as ours. Now we have a reason to head out there and escape the city."

"My mother?"

"No," he rejects quickly. "I don't want to risk dragging the press out there. I was talking about us. We're the reason."

And just like that, once again, he's giving me a reason to smile, not fret. "Cole, I just want you to know—"

His phone buzzes with a text and he grimaces. "And we're back. They found me." He leans in and kisses me. "Save that thought for when we're alone and naked." He kisses me again quickly and answers the line. "What's up, Ashley?"

He listens a minute and I don't miss the subtle tension in his body. "Okay. How the hell does this even happen?" Another pause. "Right. Yes." He disconnects and looks at me. "Somehow our arrival got out to the press. Savage is back in New York. He and some guy named Smith are waiting inside to escort us home."

"My God. This is nuts. How often do you go through this?"

"Most cases aren't televised and followed by the country, like our last one," he says. "The good news is that everyone wants you after one of these wins. The bad news is that everyone wants you after one of these wins. It'll pass quickly, but we've been out of reach. The press and naysayers need their moment. Which is why I build a security service into our fees on cases like these." He leans in and kisses me. "I'll just keep you extra close for the next week. I have more than a few office fantasies we have yet to act out." He doesn't give me time to respond. Instead, he unhooks my seatbelt and grips my waist with a gentle squeeze. "Let's go home and get naked, fuck, and then sleep for twelve hours."

"Yes, please, to all," I say, my weary body warming with the idea of finally being back home with this man. He kisses me, unhooks his seatbelt and stands up, offering me his hand.

We start walking down the ramp when his phone buzzes with a text and his jaw sets hard. "More trouble in the Houston office." He shoves his phone into his pocket. "I need to fix that mess once and for all. It shouldn't be this damn hard to run a satellite office."

"More power struggles with the partners?"

"Yes. Rumors of some sort of hostile takeover yet again."

I stop walking. "You have to get on a plane and go there now. You have to deal with this."

"We have clients coming in tomorrow to see us," he says.

"I'll handle it. Trust me to handle it." Several people walk around us.

Cole kisses me and wraps his arm around my shoulders, setting us back in motion. "I do, but if I'm forced to go to Houston this week, it will not be good for those tempting fate." His phone rings again and he glances at the number. "Savage," he tells me, taking the call.

The two of them arrange where to meet and by the time they hang up, we're approaching baggage claim. We exit the main airport to find Savage waiting for us, and every time I see the man I think of a woodsman, complete with a plaid shirt and ax. Except he never has a plaid shirt and ax. He's just big, broad, with a goatee, and a scar down his cheek, and definitely dangerous looking.

"How the fuck was Rome?" he asks when we stop in front of him.

I laugh. "Paris," I correct.

"Right," he says. "I don't like Paris. The women eat snails and raw meat. Hard to kiss a woman that has that shit in their mouths."

Cole and I both laugh. "You are a piece of work, man," Cole murmurs. "How bad is the press?"

"Not here," he says. "Because we tricked them into thinking you were on a private jet at another location. Don't ask how. We're just that good."

"I need to go to the ladies' room," I say. "Am I safe to go?"

"All is clear here in baggage claim," Savage says. "Just come right back. No detours."

I nod, relieved that the situation isn't one that requires escorts to the bathroom. Obviously, Cole was just on edge on our way home, feeling all kinds of things that he's not used to feeling. I kiss his cheek and follow the bathroom sign. Thankfully there isn't a line and I quickly do my thing, wash up and head for the door when suddenly, a burly man is in the bathroom, stalking toward me.

I scream and turn to run, but there is nowhere to go but a wall or a stall where I will end up trapped.

CHAPTER FIVE

Lori

The man coming toward me is big, charging at me, and my heart is in my throat. I can barely think. I have no weapon. I have no place to go. That's all I know until I hit the wall and the man stops in front of me, fisting his hands next to my head. Now he's so close, that I know his eyes are green because of course, I want to know the color of eyes my killer has. His face is pudgy, his arms thick with muscle. "They should have the death penalty for people like you who get killers off to kill again."

"I don't defend guilty people," I say, because if I'm going to die, I'll die fighting, be it with words or a knee. And that's what I do. I knee him, I do it with every force of energy I possess. He grunts and buckles forward, but not before he grabs a chunk of my hair.

"Bitch," he hisses, and in hindsight, his tight yanking at my scalp makes the knee seem like a mistake.

It's right then that I hear, "Lori!"

At Cole's voice, I suck in air, but the man yanks me hard against him. Cole must grab him because he's jerked backward but still has a hold on me. I'm now so close to this beast of a man's face that I see the moment Cole's fist slams into his cheek. The man releases me, and I hit the wall as he whirls and punches Cole. I scream, terrified for Cole, but in another ten seconds Savage has grabbed my attacker from behind, head-locked him, and somehow manages to speak into an earpiece, "Baggage area ladies' bathroom, now." The guy starts to flail around and sink to the ground. *Savage is putting him to sleep*, I think.

Cole grabs me and pulls me to him. "Are you okay?" He buries his face in my neck.

"I am now," I whisper, holding him as tightly as he's holding me. "I'm okay now that you're here."

"Listen up, you two," Savage says from behind us, and we turn to find the man now passed out on the floor, while Savage puts some sort of plastic cuffs on him. "Are you okay, Lori? Do you need medical care?"

"No," I say. "No, I'm just shaken."

"We're going to need to talk to the police," he says. "Smith will bring security with him when he gets here. Chaos will erupt. Stay with him or me and we have extra men on the way." He's barely spoken the words when two police officers, and a tall man with sandy brown hair I soon surmise to be Smith, enters the bathroom. From there, it's exactly as Savage said. Chaos. The man, my attacker, is taken away, and the EMS team that arrives checks our injuries, which for Cole includes a huge gash down his cheek. We're asked a million questions by a million people, and at some point, I calm down enough to start to worry.

"My mother," I say, talking to an officer. "Is my mother in danger?"

Cole turns me to face him, hands on my shoulders. "Savage has a man on the way to stay with them just to be safe."

"We think this guy acted on his own," the officer, a tall, redheaded man with such hard features that even his freckles manage to be intimidating, interjects. "He's got a relationship with the deceased on the trial you just worked."

This shakes me. A random person attacking me was less intimidating than someone who personally sought me out, but what cuts me, is that this man didn't attack me out of insanity, not literally. He's in pain. He's lost someone he loves.

"Cole," I breathe out, and he knows just what I'm thinking. I see it in his face, in the softening of his eyes.

"I know," he says softly, confirming that understanding, and wrapping his arms around my shoulders to pull me close, his focus returning to the officer. "We're going to need an emergency restraining order for us, our business, and a laundry list of people attached to this."

"I'll take the lead to push it through," the officer offers.

"What's his history and your assessment of him as a future problem?"

"He's actually a civil engineer who's been on the job ten years. He has no priors. He has no alerts on his record."

"What's his relationship to the deceased in the trial in question?"

"Brother."

Brother. That cuts me. His grief cuts me. I delivered the closing that launched my career with this case, and in his eyes, I'm the one who set the killer free. Only he wasn't a killer. "Our client needs to be alerted of trouble. He'll be a target."

"We've tried to reach him by phone," the officer says. "We have a car being sent to his residence to ensure he's well." He reaches in his pocket and hands Cole his card. "For the restraining order and if you need me."

"Can we go now?" Cole asks.

"Of course."

Cole turns us away from the officer and Savage is waiting a few feet away. "Has Reese been notified?" Cole asks the minute we're in front of him.

Reese, I think, *of course*. He's Cole's partner. He could become a target.

"Yes," Savage confirms. "Our team alerted him. He and Cat are going to meet you at your apartment. We have a vehicle waiting just outside the door."

We head that direction and I swear when we step outside, I feel like bullets will fly, which is silly. This was one man in the midst of protestors. It's over. Cole helps me into the back of a black SUV and the minute he joins me and the door shuts behind him, he pulls me to him. "You scared the hell out of me," he murmurs before his lips come down on mine, and he's kissing me like he's trying to breathe me in, like he might never kiss me again.

The front door opens and he tears his lips from mine, pressing his cheek to mine and whispers, "You will not leave me. Ever." The depths of that guttural, illogical demand that is about death, and nothing but death, ripples through me with heartache and pain.

My hand settles on his face and I whisper, "Same goes for you," but when he pulls back and looks at me, the depths of torment in his eyes tell a story, and it's not one I've heard. There is more to Cole's worry and fear.

Something that triggered his instincts before we came home, and that's clearly what happened. He felt something was coming.

We settle into the seat side by side, our legs pressed together, and Cole wraps his arm around my shoulder, holding me close. He and Savage talk, and I hear every word they speak, but my mind is on Cole, not me. Cole, not that man. There's something I don't know and it's cutting him right now; deeply and in every possible way. I'm worried about the man I love, not me, and this has me lacing my fingers with his and holding on tight.

It's a full forty-five minutes later when we enter our apartment building, which is thankfully free of protestors. I step into the elevator with Cole on one side of me and Savage on the other, but I'm still not thinking about me and my attack. I'm thinking about Cole. It's really then that I realize that this is how I felt with my mother. I left law school to protect her. Now I want to protect Cole, but the difference is that back then my mother couldn't protect me. Now, Cole wants, needs, and can protect me, while I just want to do the same with him. I need time alone with him. I need to talk to him. He needs this, too.

None of us speak on the ride up or the walk to our apartment, and the minute we're at the door, it opens and Cat is pulling me into a hug. "Thank God you're okay." She pulls back to look at me. "Are you okay?"

"I'm fine. I'm good."

She gives me a skeptical look and covers my hand with hers, dragging me inside the apartment where Reese is hovering, looking big and brooding in black jeans and a T-shirt. "You okay, Lori?" he asks.

"I'm okay," I say again. Everyone wants to know if I'm okay. I just want Cole. Alone.

"Lori," he says from behind me.

I turn and his hands come down on my shoulders. "Reese and I are going to take care of the emergency restraining orders. Stay here with Cat and Savage."

"Savage needs to go with you."

"Smith is going with us," he says. "I want Savage with you."

I have no idea when this was decided, but I don't like it. "I saw what Savage did in that bathroom. He needs to go with you."

Savage clears his throat. "Smith is a badass," he says. "He'll kick ass if he needs to."

"Can I see you alone?" I ask Cole.

"I need to go do this," Cole says. "Let me go and just get back."

"Please, Cole. I need to see you."

His jaw sets hard and he takes my hand, leading me down the hallway, past Reese and Cat, guiding me through the living room and into the kitchen. The minute we're inside, alone, I whirl on him, grabbing his belt buckle. "Talk to me."

"What does that mean, Lori?"

"Exactly. You are not you right now. You weren't you in our final moments in Paris last night. You're out of your own head."

His hands slide under my hair, to my neck. "My wife was just attacked. Right now, the only place my head is, is making sure that man never gets close to you again."

"I know, but—"

"No buts. I need you to stay here and do what Savage says. He'll let you know the minute his man has your mother in his sights. They won't approach her and freak her out. They'll just watch."

"Cole—"

His mouth comes down on mine, and suddenly I'm pressed against the refrigerator, his big body framing mine, and he is kissing me, a deep passionate, tormented kiss that is darker than any kiss I've ever experienced with this man. It's pain and torment that didn't just happen today. It's more, it's something he's never let me see and I don't understand.

"I love you," he says when he tears his mouth from mine. "I'll be back soon." And then he's gone, exiting the kitchen and leaving me staring after him.

CHAPTER SIX

Lori

I'm still standing in the kitchen staring after Cole, my heart in my throat, when Cat appears in the doorway. "Hey," she says, walking into the room and standing in front of me. "I'd hug you, but I see that look in your eyes. You're in fight mode. How about some coffee?"

"How do you know me well enough to see that?"

"We've worked together and spent a lot of hours talking in between that work," she says walking to the pot and holding up a pod. "Chocolate, right?"

"Yes," I say, smiling with the warmth of this friendship that I so needed in my life. Like I needed Cole, and Cat and our connection led me to him.

I walk to the fridge, grab my favorite creamer, which is hers as well, and sit down. She places my brewed coffee in front of me and starts her own. "What's going on?" she asks. "Well, aside from a crazy person attacking you in a bathroom, because I don't think that's what's on your mind right now."

I pour creamer in my cup. "Cole is worrying me. He's not handling this well."

"He's worried about his wife." She grabs her cup and sits down across from me. "That's called love," she adds, taking her turn with the creamer.

"I know," I say. "But this is not the Cole I know. He's tormented. He was tormented before we left Paris with just the idea of trouble and yet he says the threats and picketing are normal with one of these high-profile, controversial cases."

"Oh it is," she says. "You should have seen the insanity at the trial Reese was on when we met. It was nuts."

"And yet Cole is going out of his mind. He seems calm, but he's not. And he sent my mother away."

"That was for you. He knows how you worry about her."

"He's not good, Cat. He will lose his mind if anything else happens."

"Men like Reese and Cole are protective," she says. "It's not a bad thing. They both know how to balance that out in the right way."

"You're telling me that Reese loses his mind over picketers?"

"This is more than picketers."

"He was like this before the attack," I remind her.

She sips her coffee, her expression thoughtful. "Reese has siblings and family. They're a mess, but he has that family unit. Cole doesn't. His father doesn't count. They had no relationship at all. Just throwing this out there, but Cole has been alone a long time. He cut himself off and then fell for you in a big way. He went all in, all walls down."

"I know he did," I say, my heart squeezing. "Even when I didn't because I was scared."

"Well, it's his turn to be scared. Sometimes we think that alone is better. We can't get hurt. Then we discover alone isn't better, but losing the person who made you see that, is terrifying. I feel it sometimes. Reese puts himself on the line and I want to pull him back and keep him just for me."

I flashback to Cole telling me that we're dealing with his demons now. That's my answer. "We were living my fears before we got married," I say. "Now we're living his."

"It seems so, but his fears are all about loving you. Just love him. Listen to him. Make him talk so you can listen to him. You'll be okay."

"Thanks, Cat. I needed this."

She studies me a minute. "Let's talk about you. You were attacked."

"I'm fine. Maybe it hasn't hit me yet, but I'm fine. Did you hear he's the brother of the victim in our case?"

"Yeah. That's rough. He just wants justice."

"It makes me want to find the real killer. We tried, though, and we couldn't nail it down."

"Well," she says. "I'd say we could write a book about it together which always pressures the police, but Cole will lose his mind. It would just bring more attention to you and me. Reese might lose his mind, too."

"Maybe if we let some time pass?"

"Maybe and we could secretly work on it on our own if we're careful. I don't mean keeping it from our men, but rather, keeping it from the public."

"I love that idea."

We chat about that idea for a few minutes, which turns into an hour and a half, with no word from Cole and Reese, which has us moving upstairs where Cat helps me unpack. Actually, Cat is lying across the bed watching me, but company counts as help. I'm just pulling out the sexy lingerie I bought in Paris from my suitcase to show Cat when a realization hits me. "I haven't started my period."

She sits up. "What? How late are you?"

I forget the suitcase in front of me on the floor, and bolt to my feet. "Only one day, but I'm never late."

"You are too," she reminds me. "That's how you ended up on the pill."

"But now I'm on the pill and I'm never late."

"I'm on the pill," she says, "and I've been late. I even missed once."

"Really?" I say, feeling a small pinch of relief.

"Yes. Really. And you're only one day late."

"I know," I say, "but I was in Paris. The time zones were weird. I struggled to take it at the right time."

"Exactly. You were in Paris. Your body is all whacked out from travel and the time change, not to mention you were attacked."

"Right, but Cole is not good right now. I don't want to freak him out with this."

She stands up and settles her hands on my shoulders. "You're overreacting, which is not you. I think you're more freaked out over the attack than you realize. You're suppressing it and a crash is coming. Let's drink some wine and lay down. Maybe you can fall asleep."

"I'm not drinking wine. What if I'm pregnant?"

"You're not pregnant, but fine, we'll turn out the lights, talk, and try to snooze a bit while we wait on the men.

Actually, why don't you go take a hot bath? I'll chill out here in the bedroom."

I nod and head to the bathroom, running the water and sinking into the tub. Cat pops her head in when I'm neck deep in bubbles. "Wine?"

"No!"

She laughs and disappears, calling out, "You're not pregnant!"

I sigh. I hope not. Not now. It's not the time. Cole and I need to find us first and decide if we want to be parents. I just need Cole right now and I think he just needs me, too. I think he really needs me right now and I really wish he'd call or just come home.

I'm not sure when I fall asleep, but it's some time in the middle of a long conversation with Cat about her newest book. I blink awake and it's not Cat beside me anymore. Cole is sliding under the blankets with me, pulling me close. "Hey," I whisper groggily, my hand settling on the rough stubble of a good two-day growth. "How are you?" I ask as his big hand lands on my hip, pulling me closer, his bare leg sliding between mine that are covered in leggings I wore because Cat was here.

"Better now that I'm here with you."

"Where's Cat?"

He strokes hair behind my ear. "She and Reese headed home."

"And everything else?" I ask, catching his hand in mine, and dragging it to my chest.

"He's still in jail and we have our restraining orders. Nothing more until tomorrow."

"Cole, about you—"

"This isn't about me," he says. "It's about you."

"No. It's—"

I never finish that sentence. His mouth closes down on mine, his tongue delving past my lips, the torment he's feeling bleeding from that kiss, from him into me. I tangle my fingers in his hair, and arch into him, wanting to be closer, feeling like that is what he needs. Maybe it's what I need. Maybe I'm more rattled than I thought, because right now, I need the safety of his arms, the security. The passion that he delivers in every touch and kiss that tells me I'm alive, he's alive—we're okay.

His hands slide under my T-shirt and he pulls it over my head. I work my pants down my legs, and he kicks them away. A moment later, I'm molded against him, his mouth on mine, his tongue stroking wickedly into my mouth, even as his hands caress up and down my body. But his mouth doesn't stay on mine for very long. It travels, and he's cupping my breasts, licking my nipples, and I'm arching into him, desperate for him in some way I have never felt. He kisses a path to my belly and lingers there, and I have this crazy random moment where I wonder if his child is in my belly that terrifies me and yet—it doesn't. I think it would terrify him right now, but that thought is driven away when his mouth finds mine again, his body arching over mine, and he is hard in every possible way and place.

He cups my backside, and shifts us back to our sides, the hard length of him settling between my legs, and there is this heavy, sharper need that spikes between us. He responds to it, pressing inside me, stretching me, and then driving hard. I pant and he swallows it, and this time his kiss is all hot demand and possession. This time, we are wild, he is wild, and I taste more than torment. I taste demand. So much demand and then we are rocking and grinding and touching. We can't get enough of each other and yet we need to find that place that is enough.

I tumble over the edge first, curling into the spasms that overtake me. He holds me close, almost too tight, but not tight enough, and shudders into release. We collapse into each other, and I don't even think about getting up afterward and neither does he. I want to ask questions. I want to talk to him, but he's still holding onto me, holding me like he's afraid I'll be gone tomorrow. And so, I let him.

I want him to. And the peace I find in this is that he's dealing with whatever this is right here with me. He's not withdrawing.

And I won't let him even if he tries.

LISA RENEE JONES

CHAPTER SEVEN

Lori

I blink into the sunlight of a new day, Saturday I believe, and find Cole standing at the bedroom window, hand pressed to the glass; he's fully dressed in jeans, his impressive shoulders bunched with tension under snug a T-shirt. I sit up, his big T-shirt that I'd pulled from the suitcase after an early morning run to the bathroom, hugging my body. Throwing away the blankets, I sit up and eye the time, noting the eleven o'clock hour. Cole had been in bed with me, holding me a couple of hours ago. He wouldn't let go of me all night.

Still feeling hung over from the time change, I stand up and Cole doesn't turn. It's odd behavior, but I have no choice other than to make a quick bathroom run, and then as it is also necessary, I brush my teeth and splash water on my face. I try not to think about the fact that I still have not started my period. Cat was right. I'm stressed and there was a time change. I'm not pregnant.

Exiting the bathroom, I'm shocked to find Cole in the exact same position. He hasn't moved. I hurry toward him and when I'm by his side, I duck under his arm, stepping in front of him, my back against the floor-to-ceiling windows.

"Hey," I say, resting my hand on his chest.

"Hey," he says, his voice a rough timbre, but he doesn't reach for me.

"How are you?"

He reaches up and brushes hair from my eyes, his touch as tender as the look in his eyes. "The question is, how are you?"

I have a momentary flash of that man charging at me that I shove away. Letting that screw with my head isn't going to help Cole's state of mind. "Except for worrying about you, I'm fine. What's going on, Cole?"

"I'm meeting with the ADA handling the attack today and I might talk to your attacker. Roger Adams."

"The brother of Rachel Adams, the final victim."

"Yes," he says, "and he still thinks our client was the killer."

"He was her college professor, not her killer. The evidence showed it wasn't him."

"Agreed, but it's easy to understand how the victims' families feel. They thought justice was coming, but justice is not convicting the wrong man. It's also not attacking the attorney that forces law enforcement to do their job and find the right killer."

"About that," I say, taking what feels like an opening that might actually be good for us all. "Cat and I were talking about writing a book on the case, and trying to find the real killer."

His hands shackle my waist and he pulls me hard against him. "No. You will leave this alone. There's still a killer out there, not to mention a man in jail who could have killed you. Do you understand?" He's fierce, intense, out of his own skin.

"Cole," I breathe out softly. "I think you need to talk to me."

He stares at me two beats and then lowers his head, his forehead pressed to mine. "I found you," he says. "I'm not going to lose you."

My hands settle on his jaw. "I'm not going anywhere. We talked about this. Now tell me why this is so intense for you."

He pulls back to look at me. "Because I love you and that's new to me. Loving someone. Not wanting to lose them."

"There's more," I say. "We both know there's more to this."

He cups my face. "I tell you everything. You know I do."

"So tell me now."

"Not now," he says. "I have to meet the ADA for coffee in half an hour."

"Can you push it back an hour so I can go?"

"No," he says. "I don't want you to go."

"I'm a part of this, a big part of this," I argue.

"Too big. You're the one in danger."

"I'm not in danger anymore," I say. "You're just—"

He kisses me hard and fast. "No. I need you to do this for me. Stay here."

"On one condition," I say. "You talk to me, *really* talk to me, when you get home."

His lashes lower, and then lift. "We'll talk," he says, but he doesn't say tonight. I catch that, but I let it go.

"So Roger is still in jail, for sure?"

"Yes," he says. "I pressed the authorities to keep him there for a psych evaluation. We'll know more about his mental condition tomorrow." He kisses me. "I need to go. Savage is in the living room or I'd tell you to be naked when I get home. So, I'll undress you when I get home." He releases me and leaves.

I turn and once again, stare at the empty doorway where Cole was and no longer is. My beautiful, amazing man is broken in some way I do not understand. He's not talking to me. He says he tells me everything, but he has not and I don't know if I should push him to talk, or give him space and time. I just know that I have to decide before he returns.

<hr />

Cole

There are things I have not told Lori, but it wasn't intentional. There are things I don't think about, that until now no longer existed, thus they were not a part of who, or what, I am. Except apparently, they are. Apparently, the ghosts of my past have knocked on the door and said hello by shoving a knife into my chest.

I'm about a block from the coffee shop, when I dial Savage's boss, Blake Walker. "What kind of update do you have for me?"

"All is calm," he says. "Lori's mother is safe. The picketers apparently took Saturday off. Roger Adams is still in jail. Your client left the city. And yes, as you directed last night, we are looking for the real killer, and damn glad to do it. That lead you gave us, that tip-off about the real killer, it's solid."

"Do I need to get Lori out of town?"

"It depends on a lot of things," he says. "I would assume Roger Adams to be unstable. If he gets the help he needs, he'll be off the streets. If he's set free, the problem you have is that he might just wait you out. I'm of the opinion that you just ride it out and if he comes at you again, we'll get him locked up to stay."

"If he comes at her," I amend tightly.

"Man, I get it. She's your wife. I get it."

"And you're going to tell me you'd keep your wife here?"

"She's an ex-FBI agent that could kick most men's butts, so that isn't a fair question for me to answer. But I'm telling you my honest opinion, and I wouldn't do anything to put anyone in harm's way. Whatever you decide, though, we're here."

"Just get the killer. That ends this. I'm about to talk to the ADA and pressure him to do the same."

"We'll work with him. Just send him my way."

"I'll let you know. I'm at my meeting now. I'll call you."

We disconnect, and I enter the coffee shop, finding one man in the place at a back table. He stands when he sees me and I walk in his direction, assessing him as I go, impressed with his confidence. He's tall, with sandy brown hair, and in fit condition. He's in jeans and a T-shirt today, but still commanding. All good things. I want someone who catches a killer and puts him in jail, not something I feel every ADA I meet is capable of doing.

I cross and he offers me his hand. "Lance Miller," he says.

"Cole Brooks, and I'll say it's good to meet you after you tell me what you're going to do about Roger Adams, among other things."

"Understood," he says, meeting my eyes, no flinch whatsoever. Also a good sign. He has a backbone.

We sit down and he says, "Look. Let me just start by saying, I didn't agree with charging your client. Off the record, my boss responded to the fears that we had a serial killer and rapist. The incidents stopped when your client was arrested. That's what I'm up against. He still thinks your man is the killer."

"So unless someone else dies, you just walk away," I snap.

"Give me something to reopen the case. I'd love to slam dunk this. You know that's a feather in my cap morally and professionally and if I didn't give a shit about catching the right people, I'd be in private practice making the big bucks like you."

"You can still fight for the right side in private practice. If you choose to fight for free, that's on you." I move on. "Roger Adams."

"You know what I'm going to say."

My lips press together. "His record is clean and his attorney is good. He'll claim grief got the best of Roger and he will get out."

"But you'll keep your restraining orders," he says as if that's a comfort.

"In other words," I say. "Unless I solve this crime for you, my wife will need to look over her shoulder for the rest of her fucking life." I stand up and I don't say another word. I turn and leave, yanking my phone from my pocket.

I dial Reese. "Your ADA is a pansy-ass scared little puppy that bows to the DA."

"His hands are tied. He's really a good guy."

"What are the chances Cat will do a write-up on the entire mess and put some pressure on them?" I ask, knowing her column is widely followed.

"She already wrote it," Reese says. "Waiting on your approval in your inbox."

"I'll read it and I need to talk to Lori first. I want to get her out of town before it hits. I'll take her to Houston with me and we'll clean up that mess."

"Sounds like a good plan. Call me."

We disconnect and I start walking, knowing very well that I need to talk to Lori. I have no choice. I'm not myself and I'm not going to be myself until this is over. I love the fuck out of that woman, as Blake said of his wife. I just don't really know what to say to her. This is just my own personal demon clawing its way to the surface. I need to beat it down and beat it down now. For her. For us. And so, I walk faster, not even sure where I'm going. I'm just not ready to see Lori and yet, all I want is to see Lori.

CHAPTER EIGHT

Lori

I don't know how long I stand at the bedroom window replaying every moment with Cole since that last night in Paris, reliving every tormented, erotic moment; looking for some clue to what has set him off, all too aware it started the minute he found out there was trouble here at home. I finally shake myself into action and make it to the shower, for no reason other than I want to be ready to talk to Cole when he returns.

I hyper focus on picking out my clothes to calm my mind; I settle on outfit number three, and dress in dark jeans, and a navy V-neck tee, with navy Converse, a decision that becomes ridiculously complicated. I've just finished flat-ironing my hair and applying a light touch of make-up and lip gloss when my phone rings and I all but jump out of my skin. I grab it, hoping it's Cole, but it's Cat. "Hey, you," she says. "How are you?"

"I'm okay. Cole is not. I'm not sure what to do, Cat. He's really in alpha, protect-me mode, but it's—I don't what it is. He's just not himself."

"He called Reese and asked me to do a write-up about the case, and pressure the DA to find the real killer on your case."

I walk into the bedroom and sink into the chair in front of the window. "I guess I now know how the meeting with the ADA went."

"As far as they're concerned, you got a guilty man off. There is nothing more they can do."

I puff out a breath. "Except he was innocent and the real killer is still out there." I sit up straight. "Which is why you can't write that article. What if the real killer gets fixated on you?"

"I covered this entire case while it was happening. For me to demand a real answer would absolutely be in line with what I do. I'm handling it by way of me reporting a tip I received."

"I know you covered the case, but calling on the DA to hunt down someone who thinks they got away with murder is a whole other story."

"I called for that the entire trial," she says. "I do what I do because I have the power to make a difference in ways just like this. You and Cole and even the ADA are tied up. I am the only one who can move the dial. My readership is vocal and loyal, which is an honor they have allowed me because I talk to them in an honest way. They need to hear this."

"Cat, I don't think—"

"I started writing the article before Cole even called and right now I'm almost to your place. I want you to help me put the finishing touches on it. I want to turn it in for tomorrow's publication."

"Yes, please. Come over so I can talk you out of this."

"Your hubby wants me to do it," she says, a smile in her voice. "See you soon." She disconnects.

I immediately try to dial Cole. He doesn't answer. He went to the jail to see Roger. I know he did. My mind goes to Savage and I hurry out of the bedroom in hopes he can find out. I all but run down the stairs and hear him cursing, which only serves to freak me out and quicken my steps even more. "What's wrong?" I demand, and he stands up to face me over the top of the couch.

"Sports," he says. "Sorry about that. I curse when my team wins and I curse when my team loses."

I breathe out. "Okay. I think Cole went to the jail to see Roger. Can you find out?"

"Yeah, sure. Hold on." He slides his phone from his pocket and punches a button. "Yeah man," he says to

whoever he connects to. "Where's Cole now? Got it. Later."
He disconnects. "At the jail."

"Which explains why he's not taking my calls."

The doorbell rings and I turn toward it and Savage
protests. "Don't even think about it. I already let you get
attacked once."

"That wasn't your fault."

He scrubs his two day-ish dark stubble. "Damn sure
feels like it was." He heads for the door.

"It's Cat," I call out.

"I know that as well as I knew the bathroom was clear,"
he replies. "I'll get the door. You stay here." He charges
toward the entryway.

I wait anxiously and the minute Cat appears with Reese
by her side, I focus on him. "He's at the jail. Should he be
talking to Roger by himself?"

Reese is the one cursing now. "I'll go there now." He
kisses Cat. "I'll call you when I can." With that, he's already
headed toward the door.

I press my hands to my face. "What are you doing,
Cole?" I murmur, as if he can hear me.

Cat closes the space between us and grabs my hands.
"You okay?"

"Not until he's okay. Please don't write that article. I
cannot have you end up in the line of fire, too."

"I'm not going to get hurt. We need to catch a killer. That's what we all do together. And I know Cole knows this, but there is always a risk, but it's a limited risk. Come read it." She pats her briefcase. "And then you and Savage can give me ideas."

"I'm in," Savage says, turning off the television. "I like to catch me a bad guy, always, and our team is in on this now."

"Let's go make coffee," Cat suggests.

I nod and a few minutes later I'm sitting with both of them in the kitchen reading Cat's article out loud, focused on one important section:

What is the role of the District Attorney? Is it to get a conviction at all costs, including the life of an innocent man, or is it to convict the right person? If you didn't answer "convict the right person," let me give you something to think about. If Edward Sullivan wasn't guilty, and a jury says he was not, who raped and killed those women? And can someone like that just stop killing? Statistically, the answer is no, they will not. Maybe they moved on to another city, state, or even country, but that killer is out there. What if you, or someone you love, is the next victim?

A reliable source has told me that law enforcement, and I include the DA in this category, has leads they could follow up on to catch the real killer, but they have not. That would, of course, require that they admit they attacked and ruined the life of an innocent man. Let's just face it. Even if you're innocent, if you're accused of raping and killing four women, you will always be a rapist and a killer. What do you say on a date? By the way, I was on trial for rape and murder, but don't worry! I was innocent.

We must demand that the District Attorney, and our members of law enforcement, uphold their honor to protect us, and I for one, do not feel protected. I feel naked and exposed. If you too feel naked and exposed, I challenge you to tweet, call and even visit the offices of the people I will list out at the end of today's entry of Cat Does Crime. Until tomorrow, stay safe —Cat

"That's damn good and accurate," Savage says. "Too often the politics of an organization win and the DA just wants to calm the public and ensure election year goes well. It's an effed-up mess."

Cat looks at me. "Well?"

"You're saying 'look at me' to a killer."

"I disagree," she says, "but hey. If Reese wants to take me to Paris to get me out of town, like Cole just did you, I'm in." She scoots her MacBook to the side. "Let's talk about the suspects."

"For what purpose?" I ask, growing more and more concerned about her putting herself on the line.

"For the purpose of my team following up," Savage says, glancing at Cat, clearly thinking what I'm thinking as he says, "Right, Cat? Because this article is enough. We'll take it from there."

"Correct," she says. "Reese and I agreed that I'd pull back after the article ignites fire for my readers." She looks at me. "Let's do what we do. Let's investigate for a book we'll write together later, after Savage and his people catch the killer."

"There was a boyfriend of one of the victims and another professor who worked with our client, teaching in the same building," I say. "We used them both in the trial to create reasonable doubt but I always believed it was the boyfriend." I look at Savage and change subjects. "Can you check on Cole?"

"He's fine," he says. "My team has eyes on him."

I stand up. "I'm going to try to call him again." I punch in his auto-dial and start to walk out of the room, but I get his voicemail. I turn to face Cat. "Can you call Reese?"

"He's not been gone that long," she says, patting the table. "Come sit. I'll order us cookies from the corner bakery and we'll stuff our faces and solve this murder so your man can stop fretting."

"Yes. Please. To all of those things."

Cole

I'm standing in the holding room when Reese is brought in to join me. "You didn't need to come."

"If you kill the guy," he says, "I'm out a new partner and that can't happen."

He steps to me, close enough to ensure anyone listening is tuned out. "You could make things worse."

"Or I could convince him that we'll find the real killer," I say.

"Or you could jump over the desk and beat the shit out of him like I would if he attacked Cat, and end up in jail yourself."

"It would be worth it."

"No," he says. "It wouldn't. We'll take this on together, man. You and Lori are family. We'll do this together."

Family. He hits about ten nerves with that statement, a few I didn't know still existed until that bathroom, until I saw that man charging at my wife. "Lori is my wife."

"And our family," he argues.

The door buzzes and we both turn to face the guard. "He said to tell you that the only place he'll see you is a dark alleyway and 'fuck you.' And yes, I'll write up a sworn statement to that effect, but you shouldn't be here. You need to leave."

"We're leaving now," Reese assures him.

My jaw clenches and I look skyward, not sure if I really wanted to talk to that man or beat the shit out of him. I'm pretty sure the latter. Yeah. The latter. I was going to hurt him. I *want* to hurt him. I grab my briefcase and head for the door and I don't stop until I'm exiting the building with Reese quickly stepping to my side. "My car—"

"No," I say glancing over at him. "I'm walking. I need to clear my head."

"Talk to me, man."

"I need to clear my head."

"Cole, stop."

Fuck. I stop and face him. "I need—"

"I get it, but this is you and me. What is going on in your head?"

"Nothing good fun and fucking my wife won't solve, preferably in the opposite order, but not yet. I need to think. I love you, man, but give me some space."

He studies me a moment and reluctantly, it seems, he nods. "You know where to find me."

"I do," I say and I start walking again.

Lori

Two hours after Reese went after Cole, he returns, without Cole. Savage collects him from the door, and he joins us in the kitchen. "He's clearing his head. He'll be back soon."

"What does that mean?"

"He'll be home soon," he assures me, but he isn't home soon.

Two hours later, I'm still in the kitchen with Cat, Reese, and Savage, working the clues to the murders, but I'm barely hearing anything they say. I'm about to try to call Cole again when the front door opens and closes. I am immediately on my feet and before I can even leave the kitchen, Cole appears in the doorway, the lines of his handsome face, strained and hard.

His eyes meet mine, and I can't read what I find there when I can always read Cole. "I need to be alone with my wife," he says, his eyes never leaving mine.

There are murmurs of agreement and Reese motions to Cat to follow him. Everyone disappears from the kitchen but me, and I quickly pursue. By the time I'm in the living room, Cole is joining me, lacing his fingers with mine to walk us to the couch where he sits down and drags me on top of him. He doesn't speak, he just tangles his fingers in my hair and says, "I have something to tell you." But he doesn't tell me. He kisses me. A deep, dark tormented kiss that says more than words.

He has to tell me, but he doesn't want to.

CHAPTER NINE

$\mathcal{L}$ori

Cole is still kissing me and I cannot breathe for the emotion in this kiss, the hunger, the torment. It bleeds into me and I feel as if he is bleeding and I don't know how to make it stop. I want to ask questions. I want to demand he tell me what is wrong before I explode with fear of what it might be, but that's not what he needs in this very moment. I sense this, too. He needs me to wait. He wants to tell me. He's said he's *going to tell me* what this is, and I trust this man, with all that I am, I trust this man.

His fingers tangle in my hair, his tongue licking, stroking, and I slide my hand under his T-shirt, pressing my palms to his warm skin pulled taut over hard muscle. He reaches behind him and pulls it over his head, and already he's stripping mine away as well. I'm left in only my thin black lace bra and his gaze lowers to the swell of my breasts over the lace and then lifts. "You aren't going to ask what I want to tell you?"

"Are you ready to tell me?"

"No," he says, his voice a rough timbre. "I'm not."

"Then why would I ask?"

He slides his hand behind my neck and kisses me, a deep slide of tongue before he says, "God, I love you, woman. You are never what I expect."

"Is that good or bad?"

"I married you, didn't I?"

"Yes which means whatever it is, it's ours to deal with now. You know that, right?"

"But I didn't want it to be yours," he says. "I didn't."

"I know, but—"

"You don't know," he says, and then he is kissing me again, a drugging, intense possession, and I don't even know where he begins and I end. I sink into the moment, into this man that I love so very much, and time sways and shifts. I don't know anything but his lips, his touch, his taste. I don't even know how my bra disappears, only that it's gone and he's pressing my hands to his knees behind me, as I continue to straddle him. His fingers splay between my shoulder blades, bracing me, holding me, his other hand palming my breast, while his lips, teeth, and tongue tease my opposite nipple. He is everywhere, consuming me, and I want to reach for him, to touch him, and he seems to react, his hand sliding away from my back, forcing me to hold myself up or fall. I'm at his mercy, and I don't know why, but I am certain that this is what he needs right now. This is about trust, mine in him and his in me. And it's most definitely about control. He wants it. He needs it. He's trying to find his way back to it. With me, in this moment, he has it. When we're like this, he always has it.

He continues to tease my nipples with his mouth, his fingers, even his teeth; he's relentless in all that he does, his hands roaming up and down my body, my back, my sides, my belly. His mouth the same, and then back to my nipples, until I'm panting out, "Cole," in desperation, a plea that I don't even know how I want answered.

He drags his mouth to the hollow between my breasts, his lips pressing there, lingering for eternal moments. His eyes lift to mine, and in that breath, and the beats that follow, he is somehow dark, edgy, out of himself, and yet, so very tender at the same time. There is love in this look, in this touch of his lips. There is torment. There is regret that I want to understand. I want to take away his pain and there is so much pain that I never knew was in this man.

I am lost in everything he is, and we are lost in this moment when he drags me to him, his hand on the back of my head again. He kisses me, a tease of his tongue against my tongue, before he sets me on the ground in front of him, his hands on my hips. "Undress," he orders softly.

There's no part of me that resists a command from Cole, not like this, not when we're alone, naked, and just us. Not when I feel how much he needs me to just accept what he needs. I reach for my pants, even as I toe off my sneakers, wasting no time ridding myself of my jeans, and when I would reach for my panties, Cole stops me. His hands come to my hips and he turns me to face the other direction. "Now take them off," he orders.

I suck in air, a mix of heat and awareness rushing through me. We're back to control; Cole spinning out of control. Right now, he needs what he doesn't have. He needs that control. And so, I willingly do as he says, dragging the silk down my hips, and letting it pool at my feet, where I kick them away. With that control thing in the air, I expect Cole to keep me this way, my back to him. I expect him to spank me, or bend me over, or something that doesn't happen. His hands come down on my waist, and his teeth scrape my hip before he's turning me to face him and dragging me into his lap, my legs straddling his hips.

Once I'm there, he's kissing me, a drugging, intense, burn-me-inside-out kiss, that is forever and not long enough. Suddenly he's pressing me backward again, my hands on his knees, my breasts thrust high in the air, and his eyes raking over my naked, exposed body. The look in his eyes is as hot as they are tormented. He drags his hands over my breasts, down my waist and then his fingers are between my legs, stroking my sex, exploring and teasing, and I cannot reach for him, or once again, I will fall. Now, he has his control again, completely, fully, and I have none, yet I am sinking into this sweet blissful place that he can take me but refuses. He strokes and teases, taking me to the edge, my breathing ragged, my hips arching, and then he pulls back just enough to torment me.

He doesn't let me come. He drags me to him, his cheek to my cheek, his lips at my ear. "You come with me inside you." And then he is kissing me, a deep claiming kiss that shifts from possession to passion, to wild, hungry need. His hunger, his need, and it feeds mine.

There's a band of tension wrapping us that seems to snap. Suddenly we're all over each other; touching, kissing, trying to get closer to each other and I don't even remember how Cole's pants get down, just finally, good Lord *finally*, the hard length of him is pressing inside me, filling me, stretching me, every nerve in my body on fire. I sink down his shaft until I have all of him, and for just a moment, we don't move, our mouths lingering close, breath mingling. Cole's torment is back, waving between us, and I know in this moment, Cole feels like he will lose me. Maybe it's that he fears I'll die. Maybe it's that he fears whatever he tells me will change us, and there is only one way I can answer. I press my hands to his face, and my lips to his lips, silently reminding him that I am here in every way. He covers my hands with his and claims my mouth, and just like that, we are kissing again, the snap of tension back, and already we trying to get closer and closer, and still, it is not enough.

I'm consumed by this man, in how he feels, how he smells, how he needs and I need too, and it drives me toward that sweet spot I both want, and do not want—not yet. I try to hold back, I try to wait, to stay in this place with Cole, but it doesn't work. I, in fact, do not have control. My body clenches and then begins to spasm around Cole, every part of me trembling as I tumble into that perfect sweet moment. Cole holds me tighter, shuddering into release, a low, raw masculine sound groaning from his lips. It lasts forever and yet, it is over far too quickly. We collapse into each other, our breaths rasping in the air, melding, seconds ticking by eternally when reality returns and I realize how snugly Cole is still holding me.

Cole seems to realize this as well. He seems to come back to the present with me, his hold easing. He inches back, and strokes hair from my face. "Let's put some clothes on or I'm going to just fuck you again and not talk about this." He doesn't give me time to reply. He grabs his shirt and drags it over my head. The minute my arms are through the sleeves, he stands us up and sets me on my feet. The shock of him pulling out is more than usual. It's like a disconnect, a foreboding feeling I can't even explain.

I force myself to step away from him, and we both do what we need to do to pull ourselves together.

Cole pulls the coffee table closer to the couch, and then his hands are on my waist. "Let's sit," he says, and I settle on the couch with him on the table right in front of me, his hands on my knees. "There is something in my past that isn't another woman, or some criminal activity. It's just something that affects me. Something I didn't know still affects me this badly, but it does and that means it affects us."

My hands cover his. "Whatever it is, we can handle it."

"It affects me."

"I know. I see that."

"I don't want it to have this kind of control over me. I don't want it to fucking have this control. It will affect how I am with you. At least, until I shove it back in a box."

"I don't understand what that means, but I want to. And we'll deal with it."

He looks skyward, as if he is staring at a million stars above that do not exist, as if he's in a sea of the darkness, trying to climb out. And all I can do is hold my breath and wait until he's ready.

CHAPTER TEN

Lori

Cole and I are still sitting facing each other, him on the coffee table, me on the couch, his hands on my knees. He's looking skyward, battling his demons that are now my demons. I think that is the problem, among others. He doesn't want them to be mine.

My hands come down on his, silently telling him that I am here, and whatever this is, we'll deal with it. My touch seems to pull him back out of whatever hell he's in, and he looks at me. "I went to the jail to talk to the man who attacked you, but he refused to see me."

I'm not sure Cole should have even gone there, not in this state of mind, but I don't let myself react. He's as cool under pressure as anyone I've ever known and this is leading somewhere. I need to give him space to take me there. "He blames us for handing the man he believes killed his sister freedom. Are you surprised?"

"Yes, actually," he says, his tone sharper. "He came after my woman. I thought he'd want to taunt me. And I thought despite that, I'd make him see reason, explain our client wasn't the killer. I told myself I'd do that because it would help keep you safe."

"But?" I prod gently.

"It's a good thing he didn't see me, Lori." His voice roughens, his expression turning all hard lines and brute force. "I would have beaten the shit out of him and gone to jail without any regrets."

"No," I say, rejecting this idea. "You would not have. You know that's not the way—"

"It doesn't matter what I know," he says, his voice vibrating with anger. "When I walked into that holding room, I wanted one thing. That man's blood. Reese knew, too. He was trying to talk me off the cliff."

I swallow hard, hating where my mind goes, but it seems obvious. This is not Cole, except now he has me. "Because I do this to you," I say. "Because, like I said once before, I'm the poison that—"

"Don't go there, Lori," he says, taking my hand. "I can't have you go there right now or ever. This is not about you. This is about me. You're *everything* to me."

"But?" I press, the question rasping from my dry throat, urgency building in my belly. "Because there is obviously a 'but' hanging between us and you're starting to kill me here. Just tell me, Cole."

"There is no 'but' to us, Lori. No question between us. This isn't about us. Not in that way." He cuts his gaze and then looks at me again. "I don't talk about this," he says. "I haven't told anyone this my entire adult life. Just you. This is not for Reese. This is not for Cat. *Just you.*"

"Just me," I whisper. "Just *us.*"

"I shut this out to the point that it wasn't a problem. Well," he runs his hand through his hair. "I didn't think it was and I didn't tell you, because—I would have. At some point, I know I would have, but I just don't reach down and touch this place freely or willingly."

"But my attack made you?"

"Yes. Yes, it did." He swallows hard and looks skyward again, seeming to struggle with control before his tormented gaze returns to mine. "When I was a teen, thirteen to be exact, my father was on a high-profile case, much like the one we just worked together. He got an innocent man off, which was admirable, back when he still had a human side. He did the work law enforcement did not. He found the real killer, and did so by following the evidence they could have easily followed."

A knot starts to form in my belly with the certainty that whatever is coming is bad. Really bad. "But something went wrong."

"Yes. Law enforcement didn't make the arrest. They were slow to look at what my father presented in court."

"The killer came after your father?" I assume.

"No, Lori," he says, his voice grave. "Not my father."

That knot doubles in size. "Who?"

"My mother. We were in a shopping mall, and she had to go to the bathroom. I was waiting on her in the hallway outside. The man, the real killer, approached where I stood, stopped in front of me, looked me in the eyes, and then gave me an evil smirk."

Tears well in my eyes and I have to remind myself that this is not when his mother died. I grip his hand so tightly, so very tightly, as he continues, "I remember ice sliding down my spine a moment before he charged in the women's bathroom, and that look he'd given me, that smirk. I knew he was going to kill her. *I knew.* I ran after him, but he was already on top of her. I jumped on his back, but he threw me against a stall and my head thundered against the wall. I tried to get up and he screamed at me to stay down or he'd kill her instead of beat her. I stayed down. I stayed down, Lori."

"What else could you do?" I lean forward and cup his face. "You were a teenager, Cole. A young teenager. You couldn't have done much of anything."

"I could have gone for help. I sat there. I was stunned and scared and—" He pulls back, his hands settling on his own knees. "I could have done something more. *Something.* I could have jumped on him again. I could have hit him. Screamed bloody murder. But no. After he ordered me to stay down, I was paralyzed."

"You were *a kid.*"

"And she was my mother who ended up in the hospital for a full week. She barely lived. Ironically, considering my father's job caused that attack, it's why I became a criminal law attorney. My way of making up for the monster I let hurt someone I love." He stands up, withdrawing completely now, and then he's walking away, standing at the window, his fists pressing to the glass, chin on his chest. I quickly follow him, slipping between him and the window, but I don't touch him. I give him space, I let him decide what he needs right now, but the picture is far too clear.

"It was like history repeated itself. Someone you love. Another bathroom. Another man attacking."

"Yes. Exactly." He stares down at me for eternal moments. "This is a part of me I clearly suppressed. I didn't know it was still there, not in a truly reachable way. It affects me. I can't deny that now and it pisses me off. It was a lifetime ago."

"Of course it does. How can it not? Cole, it makes you who you are. It's a part of why you fight so hard for your clients."

"You don't understand, Lori. I didn't do relationships before you for a reason. I didn't see that as part of this, but it was. You're right. It is a part of who I am. I didn't let someone get close to me that could get hurt. That ex I told you about, the one that cheated—she called me emotionally detached because *I was*."

"But you're not. Not at all."

His hands come down on my waist and he pulls me to him. "Not with you. I never blinked. I never considered what was buried. It just didn't exist with you, but now it does."

My heart skips a beat. "What are you saying?"

"I'm clearly not good at fearing I will lose you. I don't do fear well. I don't do sit and wait well. I'm going to protect you, I have to protect you, starting with this case, and the present situation. You're going to have to listen. You're going to have to deal with how overbearing I'm going to be. I need you to understand."

I cup his face. "I'll be careful."

"No," he says, his hands coming down on mine. "That's not enough. You need to communicate. You can't just—"

"I know," I say. "I will. And we'll fight and as you said— fuck. But we'll make it work."

"You're strong-willed and independent, and while I love those things about you, I'm going to—"

"I know what you're going to do," I say. "Knowing why matters. We'll deal with it, Cole. This is not going to beat us."

"I'll shove it back in a box, but it's going to take time. You need to know that. I need to know you can handle that."

"I can. I will, but maybe shoving it in a box isn't the answer. Maybe it needs to be out. Maybe—"

"No. This needs to be buried. It has to be."

I swallow. "Okay. I'll help you."

He drags my hands between us. "Ending this case completely will help me. Cat's going to release her article tomorrow. I know you know that."

"You asked her to write it. I know. I was afraid it would get her the wrong attention."

"I agree," he surprises me by saying. "I regretted the request for that very reason. When I came out of the meeting with the ADA, it was with one certainty. Four women are dead and more could die and law enforcement isn't going to do anything. Using a reporter to pressure the DA isn't an abnormal action, but this is Cat we're talking about."

"And?"

"And Reese said that Cat decided to write the article before I requested she do it. Unlike me, with my past, which I did not share, they don't feel like her doing her normal job is a risk beyond anything we already do. He said she's not going to back down. This is why she does what she does. To make a difference. I need you to talk to her."

"I already tried, despite your request, Cole. She's writing the article. She's a champion of right over wrong. It's one of the things I love about her, and you. She'll be fine. This isn't like with your father where he named the killer, or I assume he did."

"He did," Cole confirms.

"This person is in hiding, and the truth is, Cat might be driving him back into a deeper hole as we speak. What option remains but to do just what your instinct said to do? We have to pressure law enforcement. And you—you can't start second-guessing yourself. If you do, that monster in the bathroom wins."

He presses his hands on the window on either side of me. "Right. *Right.* You're one hundred percent right."

"What happened to the man in the bathroom?"

"He was stabbed to death in prison the year after he was put there," he says. "Which is one of the reasons I was able to bury this so damn deeply. I didn't have to think about parole. It was over. I need this case to be over and now I have this idiot attacking you in a bathroom while a real killer runs free."

I press my hand to his heart. "We'll make it go away together. All of it."

He covers my hand with his and just stares at me, his expression so damn unreadable that I want to reach inside him and strip away the past. I'm contemplating how I might do that when he suddenly scoops me up and starts carrying me up toward our bedroom. I curl into him, reveling in the fact that instead of pulling away from me, he's pulled me closer. He's let me inside and while it felt like it took forever, it was only a few days before he opened a closed door and let me inside.

We enter the bedroom, our bedroom, and he sets me on the bed, coming down on top of me, the heavy, perfect weight of him comforting. He's here. We're here. He kisses me, and it's not long before his shirt that I'm still wearing is gone, and he's kissing me everywhere. He is tender and sweet, but when he too is naked and buried inside me, the demons of the past are right there with us, driving his every move, and the tenderness is gone, a rough, hard need in him taking control. I am right there with him, driving away those demons, or trying.

Hours later, he finally sleeps, but I don't. I lay in the darkness of our room, listening to Cole's steady breathing, thinking of the way he took control of my financial struggles and while it had seemed controlling at the time, I realize now there was so much more to those moves he'd made. He has a deep need to protect those he loves, and Cole made sure he loved no one. Until me. This moves me in ways that I thought impossible. How could I be moved more than I already am by this man? He's everything to me. But I am. And I am also certain the storm has not passed, but it will. I won't give up until it does.

CHAPTER ELEVEN

Cole

I wake Sunday morning, groggy, and to a beam of light, Lori's soft curves are pressing into my body, and my cellphone buzzes on the nightstand. I reach for it and eye the screen to find Reese's number. "What's wrong?" I ask. "Because something has to be wrong for you to call me this damn early."

"It's eleven o'clock," he says. "It's not early. In fact, I gave you time to sleep. Get your ass up."

Lori raises up on her elbow. "What's wrong?"

"What's wrong?" I repeat to Reese, letting her know that I have no answer to that question.

"Nothing is wrong," he says. "A lot is right. The ADA you met with wants to meet with Cat today."

I repeat the news to Lori. "On a Sunday?" she asks.

Reese clearly hears her and responds, "Yes. On a Sunday. Obviously, Cat's article stirred the right hornets'

95

nest. They want to explore her tips which, of course, came from you guys."

"Exactly," I say, watching Lori crawl out of bed, her naked ass in the air, which is a damn good way to wake up for the rest of my life. She rushes across the room toward the bathroom. "Why not ask us? Or better yet, just review the court proceedings?" I ask, watching Lori disappear into the other room.

"Why wouldn't he go to you?" Reese says. "Because that means admitting the answers were right in front of him. Cat is meeting with him at four. She wants to review the case with you guys, get her sources straight, and go prepared to get this case handled. Can you be here at two?"

"We'll be there. I'll have Savage join us, and give us an update on anything he can offer."

We disconnect, and I stand up, pulling on my pajama bottoms before I text Savage about the meeting. The minute I hit send, I stuff it in my pocket, and I'm on the prowl for my wife for about ten reasons, five of which require her to be naked. I enter the bathroom to find her just finishing up with her toothbrush. "What happened?"

"We're going to Cat and Reese's at two to help Cat prep for her meeting." I grab my toothbrush. "And I'm making sure I can tell you a proper good morning."

"It was pretty proper about two hours ago," she says, sitting down on the side of the tub to watch me, and as silly as it might seem to some, this act, just living life with this woman, cuts and heals at the same moment. It reminds me that she's a part of me now, and already I barely remember when she was not. I don't want to remember, which is exactly why I need today with the ADA to go well for Cat.

I give Lori a wink, and she replies with a charming, almost shy smile that brings my bad down about three notches and manages to make me hot and hard at the same time. I brush my teeth, splash water on my face, and take her hand. "Coffee. You on the island counter. Now."

She laughs. "What about the ADA?" My cellphone buzzes in my pocket. She laughs again. "And why are your pants vibrating."

I shake my head and laugh, reaching for my phone to find Savage's confirmation of the meeting, even as I pull her with me toward the stairs. God, this woman. Only she could take me from where I was last night to vibrating pants and laughter.

Lori

For the few hours that Cole and I are home, he is several shades cooler, as far as his mood goes. Though he's still all about heat and fire. In a good way. Those demons from last night are no longer front and center, but more backseat riders now. That is until we're both finally dressed in jeans and T-shirts, in a façade of casual that feels quite normal as we enter a private hire car on our way to prep Cat for her meeting. It's then that Cole withdraws into silence, his mood darkening, his hand on mine, gripping tightly.

We arrive at Reese and Cat's right at two to find Savage arriving as well, right along with his boss, Royce Walker. Royce, like Savage, is a big brute of a man, who's in his mid-thirties with long hair tied at his nape and a hard-set jaw. "Bossman is former FBI," Savage says, as Cat and Reese greet us at the door. "And he has some interesting information everyone needs to hear."

That gets everyone's attention and we quickly gather in the half-moon-shaped den in Cat and Reese's apartment, windows on almost every side of us. Cole and I take the love seat, Cat and Reese on two chairs opposite us, and Savage and Royce on the couch between us. Royce starts off the conversation and gets right to it. "Here's all you need to know for the meeting," he offers. "We sent out alerts to law enforcement and I got a hit. There was a murder/rape two weeks ago in North Carolina that matches the murder/rapes here. We've alerted the FBI, since this now crosses state lines, and they're taking a look at the cases."

"Someone is dead," I say at the same moment, Cat says, "Another murder. Oh God."

"That means the killer is presumed to be in another state," Cole says, his fingers flexing on my knee.

"And is there any solid lead on who it might be?" Reese asks as both men go for facts, while Cat and I have settled on emotions.

"To Cole's questions," Royce says, "yes. The killer is presumed to be in another state, still in North Carolina, or perhaps on the move again. And in my many years of law enforcement, I would venture to say he won't be back, especially after Cat's article this morning. He's on the move. He'll keep moving." He looks at Reese. "I'm told there's a suspect. He was a student at the college where the women were killed, and he moved to North Carolina even before the trial started."

"Can I tell the ADA this information today?" Cat asks. "Or when will the locals be informed, if they have not already?"

"They have not," Royce says. "But they will be shortly. As for today, I'll go see your ADA. I can go with you or you can sit this out."

"I'll join you," Cat replies. "I want to tell my readers I heard his vow to do the right thing, myself."

He nods and then looks between myself and Cole. "I'm sure you have ideas Cole about where this takes you and Lori." He eyes Cat. "Where are we meeting?"

Cat gives him the location and he stands with all of us following. A round of handshaking occurs before Savage says, "Great damn news." He rubs his hands together. "What's next?"

Cole looks at Cat. "Call me when this meeting is over because I'm what's next. I soft-served yesterday. Today, I'll be letting him know that we're suing the DA for inaction that endangered Lori's life." He looks at me. "And we are going to sue them."

"Agreed," I say. "Because someone else in North Carolina is dead. We're suing for that person and her loved ones."

We share a look and he wraps his arm around my shoulder, kissing my temple, and while this is not the gift of final closure, it's a start. I know that Cole will sleep a little easier tonight, and those demons of his will be a little quieter.

Hours later, I've spoken to my mother and confirmed she's safe and having a lovely time in the Hamptons. At present, Cole and I are sitting on our living room couch eating pizza when his phone rings and Cat is his caller. He places her on speaker phone. "The ADA assures us that they were already looking into new suspects."

Cole snorts. "Of course, we know that's a load of lies, but okay. I'll call him now." He says a terse goodbye with a promise to call her back and then kisses me. "I want to do this now, before the bail hearing in the morning."

"I want you to do it now. Roger, as crazy as he is, Cole, remember, what he did was what you wanted to do. He wanted to hurt someone he thought hurt someone he loved, even if he saw me as hurting his sister indirectly."

"He gets no sympathy. None. As far as I'm concerned—"

I lean in and kiss him. "Make the call."

He cups my head and kisses me before standing up and punching a number into his phone. I listen as he does what he does, the attorney, not the man, working, and he's crazy good at being that attorney. When it's done, he calls Cat and says simply, "He understands that I'm coming for them. He's going to make that clear to the DA tonight."

He disconnects and looks at me. "They're going to press to have Roger Adams held for mental evaluation."

"Then all is well."

"No," he says. "All is not well, Lori."

I stand up and walk to him, wrapping my arms around him. "It is for me. I have you."

He tangles fingers in my hair. "And you're not getting rid of me. Ever. You know that, right?"

"Promise?" I ask.

"I promise, but do you really need to ask that?"

"Death," I say, thinking of my father, and the near miss with my mother's stroke, "is a dark spot for me. Someone else is dead. It has a way of making you appreciate every moment. I think that's what we need to do Cole. We need to appreciate every moment. We need to get past this and live, every moment, now."

He lowers his forehead to mine. "Every moment, for now. Yes. We will." He pulls back to look at me. "After Monday. After I know Roger can't get out and come after you again."

"All right then. We make a deal right now. Roger is dealt with and then we, together, box up the past and seal it away. Deal, Cole?"

He inhales and blows out a slow breath. "Lori."

"Okay. Deal. I'm making it for both of us."

"Is that right?"

"Yes. That's right. Now. Let's go to bed."

His lips curve. "It's six o'clock."

"And your point?"

"That we have plenty time before we have to sleep," he replies, picking me up again and heading toward the bedroom.

And this time when he sets me down on the mattress, I shove at him, push him to his back and climb on top. Because right now, I think Cole needs to learn the same lesson he taught me; that sometimes, even when you don't have complete control, life can be pretty damn good.

CHAPTER TWELVE

Lori

Monday morning doesn't arrive to the sound of an alarm. It arrives to Cole wrapped around me, his hands all over my body, him pressing inside me. His demons are back, and while I won't complain about waking up with this man inside me, I just want to get us past this day. He is dark and wild, and there is no conversation. Not even when we've both shuddered into release. Instead, he silently leads me into the bathroom, and we stand under the hot shower together, both of us lost in our thoughts. We really don't have to voice those thoughts. He's worried that Roger will be released. I guess I should be, too. The man attacked me and I'm not sure I've really even let that sink in which is a testament to how much I love this man. He's what matters.

We soap each other up and I'm relieved when we end up laughing, his tension seeming to lift and fade, if only for a little while. And then for the first time as husband and wife, we get ready for work together. *That* is surreal, so very surreal. I walk into our closet, and pick out my clothes for today, with his clothes hanging opposite mine. Not that we haven't lived together for months, but today we are married. It's different. It's forever. I pick out a pale pink suit dress, one of many outfits Cole basically bought for me—not basically, he had a personal shopper with really amazing taste do it because he knew I wouldn't spend his money. Which is now our money, and I still can't get used to that.

I've just stepped into my dress when Cole, already dressed in a gray pinstriped three-piece suit, joins me in the closet, and stops at the built-in set of wooden drawers in the center of the closet. "Today is a lucky tie day," he says, opening his tie drawer. "And since I don't have one, come pick one and we'll make it lucky."

I pull out the pink silk tie I bought him a few weeks ago when I'd promised to spend money and buy clothes.

"Do you really think pink makes the statement I want in court today?"

"It says you're confident enough to wear pink and own it like the courtroom." I glance up at him. "And me, so yes. I say wear the pink tie."

He pulls me close. "You, huh?"

"My heart," I say, with a message I'm trying to get across. "Actually, all of me. And that still scares me, Cole. Love means you can be hurt, but it's worth the risk."

His eyes soften, understanding in their depths. "It is worth the risk," he says, kissing me. "And I will own the courtroom, just like you too own me, sweetheart."

"I should have recorded that," I tease, helping him with his tie.

We are laughing again as we exit the closet, and I add a pink lipstick to my lips to finish off my makeup while trying not to think about one little detail that could be big enough to become life-changing: I still haven't started my period.

Fifteen minutes later, I attempt to get Cole to agree to let me go to court with him, but he fights back so fast and hard that I leave it alone. He, in turn, leaves for court with Smith of Walker Security by his side. Thanks to the picketers and press, I leave for work with Savage as my escort, which means I can't go to the drugstore and buy a pregnancy test.

We arrive at the office building with another Walker employee at the wheel of the car, and to find picketers are indeed in place. "I pray an announcement about the FBI investigation is forthcoming, which should end this mess," I say.

"It's hard to say when that will happen," Savage replies. "They may want to stay quiet while on the hunt."

He's right and that's not a good thought, but I set it aside. It's all working out, and right now, I just want in the building. Our driver makes that happen and easily. He maneuvers us to a back entrance where we exit the car and end up inside the safety of the building without mishap.

Once we're in the elevator, Savage says, "Reporters make me want to breathe fire out of my ass, and wipe them all out."

I laugh at the ridiculous statement, but that's the thing about Savage. He's just ridiculously Savage and it's really quite charming. He knows how to take the edge off and when we exit the elevator I pause just outside to say, "Thank you."

"For what?"

"Everything you've done on this case and for us."

"No thanks needed. You two do good work. And if you need me, on or off the books, you both can call me. That's called friends."

"Friends," I say, and I'm oddly comforted by the fact that I have a bond with this man, that despite his humor, is a killer. And he is. I saw him in that bathroom. I know how easily he took down Roger. And I see that something in his eyes that says there is a dark, brutal side to him.

Once we're in the offices, Savage stays by my side, and we enter the executive lobby to see Maria. I introduce Savage and when we approach Ashley, she quickly offers me my pick of the donut selection, a "welcome home donut" she calls it. "American pastry," she jokes.

I laugh as she holds the box open, but I decline. "Too many French pastries. I need to run and eat right for about a week to pay for my Paris sins."

We chat a few minutes, and I really do like this woman. She was a bitch to me back at the restaurant, but she's been through hell and was an emotional wreck. I get it. It's easy to throw daggers when you feel like the world is throwing swords.

"I'll have a donut or ten," Savage says, hovering, and in about thirty seconds, he's flirting with Ashley. I escape into Cole's office where I often work now and shut the door. Where we work together, game planning, and being the team we've become.

Savage stays ridiculously close, hanging out in the lobby outside Cole's office. He and Ashley continue to flirt, because everyone seems to flirt with Savage, and I'm fairly certain this means his fling with our movie star client some time back was just that—a fling. I shut Cole's door, and dial

my doctor's office, forced to leave a message for the nurse.
I press my fingers to my temples. I've never really thought
about being a mother, not even when I thought I was
pregnant right after meeting Cole. I'm not sure how I feel
about it. I just know that Cole is struggling with this need
to protect me. I'm not sure he can shove his demons back
in that box if he has me and a pregnancy to face. Now is not
the time for this. Oh God. Please let now not be the time
for this. I want a baby to be something we talk about and
decide if it's right for us, together.

My man cannot do this now. I don't want to do this to
him now.

I dial Cat. "Any news yet?" she asks immediately.

"Not about the case, but I still haven't started my
period."

"It's been like two more days," she says. "This isn't
months. When this happened to me, I skipped completely.
I was normal the next month."

"Savage is hovering. I want to take a test."

"If you got pregnant in Paris, it's not likely to show up
yet."

"Can you bring me a test?" I ask. "Wait. No. There are
picketers." My phone beeps and I glance at the number.
"It's my doctor's office. I'll call you when I hear from Cole."
I switch lines. "Hi," I say. "I should have started three days

ago and I have not. I was in Paris, and I was late taking my pill a few times and—"

"Paris last week?"

"Yes."

"You didn't miss your period because you screwed up your pill less than a week ago. If you're pregnant it happened before that. Take a test. It should be 99% accurate at this stage."

"And if it's negative?"

"Then relax. Stress and the time change could affect your period, even on the pill."

I breathe out. "Okay. Yes. I'll take a test."

"And listen to your body. Do you feel pregnant? Some women know right away."

"I don't. No, I don't feel different. If I take a test and it's negative, then I start back on the pill like normal?"

"Yes. That will be fine."

I disconnect and decide that between trying to find a way to privately buy this test, and waiting on news from Cole, I'm going to lose my mind.

Cole

The pink tie was a good decision. It reminds me of Lori and she's what today is about. I'm about to walk into court when Reese catches me at the doorway. "I hate that I can't be in there with you, man," he says. "But—"

"You have court and a client who needs you," I say. "And there's nothing you can do in there. There's nothing I can do but pressure the ADA to do his job and let the judge see the face of Lori's husband and protector as a reminder that she was attacked."

"Call Cat when it's over and text me."

"I will."

A few minutes later, I'm sitting in the courtroom and it kills me to sit back and pray that my promise of a lawsuit gave the DA enough pause to allow the ADA the freedom to do his job. The side doors open and Roger is led into the room and I swear, every muscle in my body locks up and my fingers curl into my palms. He was smart to stay away from me. I would have beat the shit out of him. Oh yeah, I would have.

Lance Miller stands behind the prosecutor's table and surprises me by waving me forward.

"The Feds called the DA," he says. "My boss knows he fucked up now, but he's not going to admit that. He will, however, let me do my job now."

"That's good to hear," I say. "But that isn't going to shut down my legal action. Another woman is dead because your boss didn't act."

"I know that," he says grimly. "I absolutely know that."

"Are you able to speak about the FBI investigation today?"

"On a limited basis. For the safety of you and your wife, we're allowed to do so, but in the judge's chambers. If I can convince the judge to hear you speak, are you in?"

"Hell yeah," I say, "but we both know that's unlikely."

"The circumstances are out of the ordinary. If nothing else, I'm going to try to get you in chambers."

I nod and sit back down, and it's not long until we're on our feet for the judge's entry. Lance gets right to it and asks for a chamber meeting. A few minutes later, I'm called into chambers as well. Everything is smooth and fast. Roger is sent for a mental evaluation that may only buy us a few days before he's free, but his attorney has been told about the investigation. Roger will now know that the killer is not our client. His attention should shift away from our team. *Away from my wife.*

I exit the courtroom, text Cat and Reese, and then dial Royce Walker. "Where are we on an arrest?"

"The suspect is still in North Carolina and they're comparing evidence between our cases and theirs today.

They have eyes on him twenty-four-seven and they expect an arrest this week. I'll keep you posted."

I disconnect the line and I know that I need to call Lori with the good news, but I can't seem to make the call. I text her instead: *Roger is being held. Arrest pending in North Carolina. More when I get there.*

More.

That's the problem. There's more to come and I'm not sure what that more is, but it's a knot in my chest that I want to punch away. This isn't over yet. That's what my gut is telling me. I look down at my pink tie, the tie that Lori came home with after I insisted she spend money. She bought nothing for herself that day. She can't accept the freedom of just being secure and safe. I can't tell her I believe she is when I don't. Not yet.

When I tell Lori she's safe, that she finally has her fairy tale ending, I want her to know that I mean it. That it's real. And I can't tell her that yet, but as I start walking and motion Smith forward, I vow that I will. And soon. Once I tell her our world is right and perfect again, I'll live my life making sure it stays that way.

CHAPTER THIRTEEN

Lori

The next morning Cole and I wake to the news that an arrest has been made in North Carolina, a man arrested for the murders our client was accused of committing, and of course, the press is everywhere. We're fully dressed in the kitchen, me in a suit with a cream-colored blouse, Cole in a navy suit with a white shirt, and coffee cups in our hands when he finally reaches our client. "You're vindicated, man," he says. "You're free in all ways." He listens a minute. "We need to do a press conference and you'll have offers thrown your direction. We have a partnering firm Maxwell, Maxwell, and Maxwell, that can manage them for you and ensure you are well taken care of." Maxwell, Maxwell, and Maxwell being Cat's brothers, who handle corporate and contract law.

Once Cole disconnects, I sigh. "This is all pretty surreal."

"Yes. Yes, it is. And we did this together."

"And that," I say. "Is pretty special."

"Yes, it is, sweetheart. We're a good team."

Warmth fills me as he strokes my cheek, and it stays with me on the ride to the office that includes my mother calling me, excited about the case, and the arrest. I love that she has followed it. I love that she is in this with us. And of course, there is a call from Cat. "I can't believe it's over. It's surreal."

"I said the same thing."

We chat a few minutes and right before we get to the building, she whispers, "Any *other* good news?" she asks, obviously talking about my period.

"No," I say. "None. And you know shopping won't be easy right now."

"I'll grab a test. I can't get it to you today, but we're bound to end up together at our place or yours to celebrate. I'll have it ready."

"Thank you, Cat." I disconnect, and Cole gives me a curious look, but before I feel I must explain we are at the rear of the building, and it's time to exit.

From there it's pure chaos but the good kind. Everyone wants to talk about the arrest and the press conference and there is not a moment to breathe, most certainly not a moment to think about the birth control pill I don't have to start for another four days.

There's no celebration and not because we don't want to, but the rest of the day is pure insanity that just never lets up and Reese ends up with a client emergency. The closest to celebration Cole and I get is falling into bed together and actually sleeping.

The next two mornings, I'm suffocated by security and we're on to Wednesday in a blink of an eye, but the press is finally slowing down, the picketers long gone. Finally, we agree that Thursday will be Savage's last day. Freedom exists and we're even going to Cat and Reese's for a celebration Thursday night, and just in time. I have to start back on my pill tomorrow morning.

It's mid-afternoon, and I've just walked into Cole's office to review a stack of the associates' cases with him when Ashley buzzes in. "I have the CEO of Carlson Wright on the line. He's in jail accused of murder. He says he was set up by his partner, and he needs urgent assistance."

"Tell him to find another attorney," Cole says. "I'm not him."

"What?" I gasp at the same moment as Ashley.

"This is huge," Ashley says.

"Why wouldn't you at least talk to him?" I demand, forgetting Ashley is on the line and setting the files in my arms on the desk.

He looks up at me, not even bothering to stand, his eyes narrowing sharply, and he's pissed, really pissed, and I don't know if it's the challenge behind a closed door or what exactly. He just is and I am.

"We do not want this case," he says to me and refocuses on the call. "Tell him now, Ashley," he orders, "and let the man make appropriate arrangements."

"I'll tell him," she says, disappointment and confusion in her voice.

I cross to the door and shut it, walking back to his desk and pressing my hands on top to lean toward him. "Why did you just turn down that case?" I demand, but I already know. It's me. He turned it down to ensure I don't end up in the line of fire again. His demons are alive and well, in fact, they are prospering and winning.

"We do not need another high-profile press nightmare right now to create chaos for the firm."

"What about helping an innocent man?" I challenge.

"We don't know that he's innocent," he argues.

"Because you won't even talk to him," I counter.

"No. I won't."

"Explain, Cole."

His jaw sets hard. "I just did."

"In other words, when you were training me, you'd give facts and reasons, but now that I'm your wife, I just need to get it."

"Wife and employee need to understand that I've made this decision. It's done."

I push off the desk and start walking. By the time I'm at the door, his hand is on the wooden surface by my head, that spicy perfect scent of him, all dominance and man, teasing my nostrils. But I don't want him to be dominant right now. I want him to be smart. My chin lowers to my chest, my anger, and his now too, palpable. "I will make the decision I need to make to protect you."

I explode on that and whirl around to face him. "To protect me? So, should we both retire? Surely you should break up the partnership with Reese because you won't be able to bill what you need to bill to do your part. How much money did you just walk away from? For him and for the employees of this firm who want to grow, learn, and earn?" I grab his lapels. "How much, Cole?"

"We're on the heels of living hell."

"We're on the heels of a huge win. We're going to see Cat and Reese to celebrate. We're married. We're happy. This *is not* hell."

He cups my face. "I will not—"

"I resign," I say. "I quit, Cole. This is my two-week notice. I'll go to HR and make it official."

"What?" He releases me and presses his hands on the door on either side of me, his arm caging me in. "What the hell are you talking about?"

"This is your career. You love your career. You love what you do and when you stop doing it for me, you will wake up one day and hate me and us."

"That's not going to happen."

"Exactly. Because I'm going to go to work with someone else. I'm going to give you space to be you again and then we can help each other, but—"

"No," he says, his tone absolute. "We like working together. We're good together and I never thought I'd say that about anyone. I never thought I'd want to partner with anyone. You aren't leaving. Not when I know it's not what you really want."

"It is," I say. "It's what's good for you, me, us, and this firm."

"You're wrong," he says. "And I hope when you get over your anger, you change your mind because not taking this case right now, is as much about you as it is me and us. And even this firm."

"When will it be okay to take another high-profile case, Cole?"

"You haven't even dealt with the fact that you were attacked. And I haven't either. We need to fucking breathe, Lori. I'm not my best right now and neither are you. And that's not fair to the client or this firm. There will be ten offers or more in the next week. This one wasn't the one. I'll know when it is."

His phone buzzes again. "The district attorney is on the line," Ashley states.

Cole's lips thin. "And we aren't done with the last case yet or the DA wouldn't personally be on the line to talk to me right now." He pushes off the door and walks to his desk in what will obviously be a conversation about the lawsuit he's promised to file.

I don't stay. I open the door and exit without looking at Ashley, needing time to think. Was I wrong in there? Was I right? I cross the lobby, stopping to speak to Maria like normal. I enter my office and shut the door. Cole doesn't follow. Fifteen minutes later, I haven't heard from him. My files are in his office and I have no choice but to return when my phone buzzes with a text from Cole: *I'm on my way to the DA's office. I cancelled our dinner with Cat and Reese.*

I'm glad he cancelled because I'll want to talk to Cat, and if I do, I'll have to tell her Cole turned down a huge case for the firm. I would never do that. She's a friend, but she's also the wife of Cole's partner. I need to talk to my husband. I need to think. I need to take a pregnancy test. I pull up my computer screen and google: What if you take the birth control pill and you're pregnant?

Per the U.S. Food and Drug Administration (FDA), no evidence has been found that supports taking birth control pills while pregnant will harm your baby, or cause birth defects or complications.

I breathe out a sigh of relief. I don't need to take a test today. I don't need to know today. I need to talk to my husband. I dial his number. He answers on the first ring. "Are you already gone?"

"Yes. I'm walking to my meeting now. It's only a few blocks away."

"Okay."

"Okay?"

"You didn't even stop by and see me."

"Because if I walked into your office I would have shoved your skirt up, fucked you, and then left for my meeting angry anyway."

"Oh," I say.

"Oh?"

"I think I would have liked that better than you just leaving."

"You were wrong in there, Lori but that was my fault. I opened us up to this when I told you what I told you."

"Are you saying you shouldn't have told me?"

"I don't know what I'm saying. I need to think and so do you."

"I don't like how that sounds."

"I love you, Lori. It doesn't mean anything besides I love you, I have a meeting, and I need to think. I need to go." He disconnects, and I suck in a breath. Was I wrong when I challenged him? Or was I right and he doesn't want me to be right? And who can I even talk to about this? No one. I can talk to no one.

It's nearly seven when Cole finally calls. "I have a problem I need to deal with. Savage is going to take you home."

"What problem?"

"The DA offered us a settlement. I'm meeting with Gabe Maxwell, one of Cat's brothers, to negotiate the civil settlement for us, our client, and the victims' families, and unless you have a problem with it, I'd like to donate our portion to the victims' families."

My heart swells with love for this man. "I love that you want to do that."

"Good. I might be late. I want Savage to take you home just to be sure that there are no lingering press issues."

I open my mouth to argue and decide I've done enough of that today. "That sounds good."

"I'll be home as soon as possible and then we can talk."

"That sounds good," I say again. There's a voice in the background.

"I have to go, Lori. We'll talk." He disconnects, and I feel disconnected in more ways than the phone line. I need to fix that and fix it tonight.

CHAPTER FOURTEEN

Cole

I walk into the offices of Maxwell, Maxwell, and Maxwell, expecting to meet with Cat's brother, Gabe, who I know well. Instead, I'm led into Reid's office, and while the two look like a couple of blond Twinkies, Gabe is easygoing and full of humor. Reid is a hard-ass who barely smiles, let alone jokes. "Gabe is tied up with a crisis," Reid says, as I claim the seat in front of him. "You're stuck with me and while this isn't my normal area of expertise, I'll handle it and handle it well."

"I hear you're a beast," I say. "That works for me. I threatened to sue over Lori's attack, which was caused by the inaction of the DA as it relates to actually solving this case, rather than blaming an innocent man. The DA wants to settle. I want double what he offers and for the money to be split between the victims. Additionally, I want a settlement for my client. I talked to him on the way over. He's on board, if you're on board."

"I'm on board for triple the payout and I'll get it."

"That also works for me. Additionally, another woman was killed in North Carolina while the DA sat on his ass. Walker Security will connect you to the right people to include in the lawsuit. I want them to be taken care of as well. Obviously, you cash out big."

"I'll donate the money and my service to the family as well."

I narrow my eyes at him. "Really? And here I heard you don't have a heart."

"I don't," he says. "I'm just borrowing yours."

"Right. Just borrowing mine." I stand up. "It's in your hands now. I need to move on."

"Lori is safe now?"

I cut my gaze and then look at him. "Roger Adams is being committed, but for how long? So yes. She's safe... for now."

"I can apply a hell of a lot of financial pressure to ensure he's kept away from her."

"Then do it. Be the beast I hear you are. This isn't about money to me. It's about my wife."

"Understood and so you know I mean it." His eyes meet mine. "I get it. More than you know. You found her. You don't want to lose her."

In that moment, the understanding that passes between us tells me that "the beast" is a beast because he does get it. His past, while unexplained and unnamed, cuts through the air and collides with mine. I don't want anyone to understand me as well as I now believe this man does, but I find comfort in the fact that he does. He knows loss.

I give him a nod and head for the door. Now, it's time to go see my wife, who I love with all my heart, but this is definitely going to be one of those fight and fuck nights.

Lori

Waiting for Cole to return from his meeting with Cat's brother over the settlement offer is going to kill me. The apartment is empty and I'm alone in my torment. And I *am* tormented by what happened today with Cole. One part of me feels I was completely wrong, but every time I go down that path, I am reminded of his desperate need to protect me at all costs. He said that we weren't ready for another case. He didn't say the client was a bad choice. It is everything to be loved this much by someone you love, but that is exactly why I have to look out for him while he looks out for me. He's made my goals and career important, and I just don't want to hurt him in any way, ever.

Desperate to do anything to stay busy, I change into sweats and a T-shirt, and end up on the living room floor in front of the coffee table with my MacBook, a bowl of cantaloupe and a glass of wine, when I really want Ben & Jerry's ice cream. The pastries I ate in Paris say I'm stuck with the cantaloupe, but I hope to eat dinner with Cole. I jab at a chunk of fruit which I eat and wash down with wine, which is a horrible idea. The wine is now bitter. My cellphone rings and I hope it's Cole, but when I grab it where it sits next to my computer I find it's Cat calling.

"Did you take a test?" she asks when I answer. "Or better yet, did you start your period?"

"Nope and nope," I say. "And I can't seem to get me and a test in the same room, but I'm officially without a bodyguard tomorrow. I'll pick one up."

"I grabbed a couple for you because I know you'll want to test and retest the results. And of course, I thought you two were coming over. Reese said maybe tomorrow night?"

"Yes," I say. "Hopefully we can, though I'd like to take a test before then."

"Do you feel pregnant?"

"What does pregnant feel like?" I ask. "Because other than gaining five pounds, I feel the same. And I'm pretty sure I earned those five pounds in Paris by way of food, not a baby."

"They say you feel different. You just *know*. I, however, wouldn't know, because I've never even thought I was pregnant."

"Do you want to have kids?"

She sighs. "Me and Reese, mom and dad? Maybe. I mean, it's Reese. That man would make beautiful babies, but right now Reese is at the top of his career. Every case he takes is high profile and he and Cole are both superstars. It's one intense case after another, and I love watching him work and succeed. Now is the time for him to stay focused and build the firm."

"Right," I say, my throat going dry. "You're right. Now is a bad time."

"Oh God. Lori, I didn't mean this is a bad time for you to be pregnant."

"But it is. Cole and Reese came together for a reason. They're on top, and they have a firm to build." I change the subject with a hard push. "Did you hear the DA called Cole to his office?"

"Yes, and I know about the settlement and also know that you just changed the subject."

"I just need to take the test and stop talking about it and babies."

"Where's Cole now? Can you go grab one?"

"He's meeting with your brother to deal with the settlement negotiation. He could walk in the door any minute."

"If you two don't come to dinner tomorrow night, come by and read my new project. I'll have the tests waiting for you."

We chat a few more minutes and disconnect, which is a relief. I can't think about pregnancy tests right now. I can't think about a pregnancy making Cole even more crazy. I can't ruin his career because he won't take the cases he needs to take to push forward.

I need to think about what happened today with Cole. I key my computer to life and search the client he turned down today. It's not long before I find him to be a vicious killer in business, with connections to Texas, Houston specifically, which explains why he was so quick to call Cole when he was in trouble. Maybe Cole knows him or knows things about him. Maybe, but I know that wasn't the entire problem.

The door buzzes with the security system telling me that Cole is home. I don't move. I'm frozen here, and I'm not even sure why. I just—I know we're in one of those bumps in the road. We have fought them before, but this feels different. I suck in a breath and Cole appears, his tie at half undone, his jacket over his arm. He stares at me for several beats, his eyes unreadable, the lines of his handsome face hard.

He sets his jacket and briefcase on the couch and looks at me, but I'm on this side of it and he's on the other. He presses his hands to the back of the couch. "I'm staying over here so that I can talk to you, rather than fuck you, because fucking you might feel good, but it doesn't solve anything."

I swallow hard. "I would agree."

"Do not threaten me with leaving in any way shape or form. That doesn't work for me or for us."

I suck in a breath with the barely contained fury in his voice. "You mean when I resigned."

"Yes, I fucking mean when you resigned. You talk to me. You fight with me. But there is no quitting or leaving. We are either in this together all the way or not. I need to know now."

"Leaving my job isn't about leaving us."

"Isn't it? Because that was part of what we wanted. To be back at work together. To live this life together. And if you just want to do something separate because you need independence, I get it. I'll support that and you, but do not use it to manipulate my decisions. That will not go well for us."

I go down on my knees on the couch in front of him. "How can you even begin to think I was threatening you or manipulating you? That's not me. That's not us."

"You're right. It's not. So, what the hell was that, Lori?"

"You can't make decisions based on me."

"The hell I can't."

"You can't. If we're to work together, you can't. We both want to work challenging cases, high-profile cases, Cole. Any client could lead to a problem. We'd have to change professions to avoid that and even then, there could be some other risk."

"That doesn't make this moment the right moment to take that risk. I'm still negotiating a settlement for the victims. You haven't even dealt with being attacked and it will hit you. You will have to deal with it. This is *not* the right time, but putting that aside, you cannot question me at work, on the spot, in front of Ashley. Just as I won't you. That belongs here or behind closed doors and not on speakerphone or you're right. We can't work together."

"I know," I say. "I regretted that the moment it happened. I'm sorry. I'm really sorry." My hands cover his, my voice roughening with emotion. "You have done so much to support me. I just don't want to hold you back. I feel like I'm the reason those demons are out of the box. I *know* I am."

"You are not the reason. I'm the reason. I let them get the best of me, but I deal with them the same way you dealt with yours; with action. I'm taking action. I'm making people pay for what they did, for the people they hurt, including you. I'm taking this all the way to completion and when that's done, then I'll take a case, and I'll win that case. You need to decide if you want to do that on the field with me or from the sidelines." He pushes off the couch and starts walking toward the stairs.

I stare after him, stunned that he's walked away. That's not Cole, not with me. He stands. He fights, and now I'm standing, pacing, trying to understand what just happened. I replay the entire conversation and stop dead in my tracks. I used the worst tool possible to get to him today. I threatened to leave at least a part of our life, when losing me is what he's battling and while I apologized I didn't say what he needed to hear.

I race up the stairs and enter the bathroom to hear the shower running. I step into the bathroom to find Cole under the spray of water. I quickly strip and walk to the door, opening it and joining him. His hand runs over his hair, smoothing it from his face. "I shouldn't have resigned. I don't want to leave. I love working with you. I love every second. I was just worried about you. I was just—I need to protect you, too. Because that's what we do. We protect each other. Cole, I—"

I never finish that sentence. He grabs me and pulls me to him, his mouth covering mine in a passionate, hungry kiss before he says, "Don't ever say you're leaving again. Not like that."

"I won't. I promise. But promise me—"

"I won't promise not to make decisions based on you, Lori. I won't. But I will tell you that having you in my life, worrying over you, isn't a bad thing. It's everything. Like you're everything."

His mouth closes down on mine again, and with a lick of his tongue, I'm against the wall, and he's lifting my leg, pressing inside me. The fighting is over, and now the fucking begins. And that's what this is. He's driving inside me, lifting me and pumping inside me, and every angry word we've spoken today evaporates into passion and need. Into his mouth on my mouth, his lips on my lips, his hand on my breast, my nipple, everywhere. He is touching me everywhere, and when it's over, we stand under the water, our foreheads pressed together in silence, that good kind of silence that says we don't need words. We just need each other and there is a shift between us, an understanding that we can fight and we can disagree, even under terrible circumstances, but we are one, and that cannot be broken. I think in all our many separate broken pieces, we both needed to know that together, we're whole.

CHAPTER FIFTEEN

Lori

It's a long time after that shower when Cole and I sit on the living room floor with Chinese food in front of us, me in one of his T-shirts, and him in his pajama bottoms. "So, it went well with Gabe Maxwell?"

"Actually, I saw Reid, his brother."

"Oh," I say. "He's the one Cat has real issues with. She says he's a lot like her father and that's not a compliment."

"I don't know the details of Cat's relationship with her father or with Reid, but her father is, or was before his stroke, one of the best corporate financial attorneys in the business. In that light, Reid is indeed like his father."

"He has a heart. He hides it well, but tonight, I saw a little glimpse of what's beneath. He'll do right by the people we want to do right by and in a big way."

I set my fork down, seeing a chance to get him to talk about what he never talks about. "Cat and her dad, I think—well, I think they are a lot like you and your dad. He wanted her to be like him. She isn't. She never will be. They didn't speak for a very long time, but he had a stroke, and she started to rebuild a relationship, a fragile one, but a relationship."

He sets his fork down. "You want to know about my father."

"I want to know how it affects you. It's still fresh, Cole. Less than two years. I'm wondering if that box you thought sealed only opened because his death cracked it open. You were ripe for an emotional stumble. All this has to be a trigger for you. I mean—when did you start hating him?"

He inhales and lets it out. "You're right," he surprises me by saying. "His death is likely a trigger. Bastard that he is, he probably did crack open the box. He made me think about his life, my life, my mother." He moves to sit on the couch, lowering his head and running his hand over his neck.

I quickly join him, scooting close, my leg and hip pressed to his. "When my mother had her stroke right after my father died," I say. "I had this freak-out over being alone. There's just something about no longer having a living parent on this earth that still steals my breath just thinking about it."

He looks over at me. "Exactly. I hated that man but somehow the world was right when he was here for me to hate, up close and personal." He takes my hand. "As for him opening the box, how very him to try to get between us, even after his death."

I squeeze his hand. "He's not coming between us, Cole. One thing I can tell you about me is that despite my misgivings about my father, after his death I saw the devotion between him and my mother. They had good and bad times, and they worked through them. I'm not a fair-weather person."

"If you were a fair-weather person, sweetheart, you wouldn't have made the sacrifices you made for your mother. And in his own way, my father loved my mother, too. It's just not my way."

"And that means what to you? Because if you mean you wouldn't have let your mother get attacked the way your father did, he couldn't have stopped that. Not the way you've described it happening."

"That's not what I meant," he says quickly.

"You couldn't have stopped my attack either. Is that the problem? You're comparing yourself to him? Us to them? Because if you are, we're in trouble."

"Making sure I am not like him is the opposite of trouble."

"Not if that means you are holding yourself and us to standards we can't possibly keep."

"By that, you mean what?" he asks.

"The only way to stop that attack was to have never taken that case."

"If I think a case is dangerous, I need to pass it on to someone else."

"And think about what that might mean. Would another attorney have gotten that innocent man off? Would another attorney have gotten Royce Walker involved and linked the cases to help catch a killer? How many more would have died? My attack was nothing."

He cups the back of my neck and drags my mouth to his. "Your attack should never have happened."

"But it did and I'm okay because you were right there to save me." I touch his jaw. "And we saved other lives together. I should never, never have suggested I resign. I love what we do together."

"Me too, sweetheart. Me, too." He brushes his lips over mine. "I told you. I'll get by all this. Give me space without stepping away."

"That's a confusing statement."

He lowers me to the couch and settles on top of me, the soft rug tickling my legs while his breath whispers against my lips. "I love you. Is that confusing?"

"No. No, it's not."

"Just in case I didn't make that point clear, let me show you, not just tell you." He drags his shirt over my body, and then his mouth comes down on mine, and he is kissing me, a gentle caress of tongue against tongue, a kiss that is a seduction. His lips part mine and drag over my cheek, down my neck, and his hands caress my nipples; his tongue follows. And when he slides between my legs, his mouth on my belly, he lingers there, tenderness in the way his lips caress the delicate skin. His mouth travels lower, but he doesn't lick that most intimate part of me. He kisses my thighs, my knees, every part of me it seems, before yes, he licks me there, but this is not about sex. This is about making love and he doesn't linger, doesn't make me shatter under his mouth.

He presses inside me, kissing me, rocking with me, and we don't rush. We just feel what it's like to be us, to be married, to be in love. And it's a long time later when we lay on the couch with my head on his chest, his heart thundering under my ear, when I realize why tonight was so different. He faced a demon tonight, we faced a demon tonight: His father. And that must have been the biggest, or even the entire army of demons, because his demons were not with us. I had Cole. Just Cole, the man I love.

The next day, Cole and I laugh as I end up in a red silk blouse under my black skirt and jacket, and he's in a black suit with a red tie. He proclaims us a "power couple" and we head to the office in good spirits. We've barely settled into his office with Ashley to review a variety of agency business that Cole will be going over with Reese tonight, when Reese's secretary, Maria, pokes her head in the door.

"Flower delivery, Ashley."

Ashley, who is looking lovely in a floral print dress, frowns and gets up. "I have no idea who would send me flowers. We all know my love life is about as toxic as it gets. Let me just eye the card. I'll be right back." She stands and exits, and I look at Cole. "Is there any news on her ex?" I whisper. "So much happened, I never really got any details on that situation."

"The FBI got involved. She was cleared. We were all pushed out."

I glance at the door and back at him. "Cleared of what?"

"I can't even tell you that. It was that top secret, which is why I haven't said much. There wasn't much to say."

His phone rings and when he reaches for it, I decide to go see the flowers. I exit the office, glance at the stunning bouquet of at least three dozen pink roses, and then search for Ashley, who is nowhere to be seen. I eye Maria who points toward the door. Frowning, certain something is wrong, I hurry toward her. "We were in a meeting. Did she say anything?"

She leans forward a bit and whispers, "No, but I'm pretty sure she was holding back tears."

"Okay, thanks." I hurry out of the executive office, through the lobby and into the bathroom. One of the two stalls doors are shut. "Ashley?"

"Yes?" she calls out and she tries to hide her sob, but she fails.

I knock on the door. "Open up. Talk to me."

Seconds tick by and she finally opens the door, her mascara streaked down her cheeks. She shoves a mini-card at me. "Read it."

I glance down and read: *Nothing was what it seems. I promise you, baby, I love you. I'll explain. I'm coming for you just as soon as I can.* All kinds of alarms are going off in my head and I glance up at her. "What's your reaction?"

"I don't know if I should be scared, relieved, or what, really. I loved him. The idea that he lied and never loved me still guts me. But he was involved in some big international—" She throws her hands up. "I don't even know what. Cole couldn't find out what."

"Let's go talk to Cole now."

"I can't. I'm a mess."

"You could be in danger. We need to talk to Cole."

"I need a few minutes," she says, swiping at her cheeks.

"Okay. I'll go talk to him. Come find us."

She nods, and I hug her. "It's going to be okay."

"Thank you. Thank you, Lori. I have no one. I moved here from Houston and my family is gone and—just, thank you."

"You have us." I hurry out of the bathroom and run smack into Cole, his big hands catching my arms.

"I have to go to Reid's office. Ride down with me."

I nod and we step into the elevator where I hand him the card. "Holy hell," he murmurs, looking at me. "I'll make calls and find out where he is and what he is. And tell her I'm having Walker Security send someone over to look out for her for the next few days."

"She's pretty confused."

"Of course she is," he says. The elevator dings and we exit to the lobby, pausing just outside the door. "I'm going to Reese's place after my meeting. We're going to sit in the bar downstairs and pick through a few strategic moves, namely what to do about the Houston office. I'll meet you at their place for dinner. Yes?"

"Yes. That works. I'll probably head over early to visit with Cat."

"See you there." He pulls me to him and kisses me. "I'll call you if I hear anything on Ashley's situation." And with that, he's gone, and I punch the button for the elevator car. Time to go take care of Ashley, and tonight, I'll finally take that pregnancy test, which I'm not going to think about. Right now is about Ashley and her man problem.

It's after five when I leave the office, with no news from Cole. Smith, one of the Walker men who was at the airport the day I was attacked is now Ashley's shadow, which is about as taken care of as that situation gets right now.

Once I'm at Cat and Reese's apartment, my nerves over that pregnancy test have arrived, and they seem to be hopping around and doing jumping jacks in my belly. I normally would stop by the bar to say hello to Cole and Reese, but I just can't. I need to do this test. I text Cat right before I step into the elevator: *I'm on my way up. Have the test ready. I want to do it before Cole arrives.*

I step into the car, and punch the button, literally pacing the small space. Cat opens the door and holds up the boxed test. "The coast is clear."

I grab it and head for the bathroom as she yells, "I still have another box if you want to double check the results!"

"I'm going to want that test!" I reply, entering the bathroom and shutting the door, my heart thundering in my chest, my gaze locked on the words Pregnancy Test.

This is it. This is when one little pink line could become life-changing.

CHAPTER SIXTEEN

Cole

Reese and I sit in the bar, and I happily down my second whiskey when I would normally stop at one, but it's been a hell of a month, really six months, considering my move and my father's death. "We look good on paper," Reese says. "And with the high-profile cases we've both won the past year, we have offers coming in left and right."

"Meanwhile the Houston location is still a problem," I say. "We need to bring in another me over there to oversee the operation, someone we trust. Someone we make a partner. I know that's not ideal, but there's a lot of money to be made there."

"Agreed. You couldn't stay there and have us rule the world with the same vision and momentum, but with your father gone, and you shortly after, it's a ship with holes. Anyone in Texas in mind?"

"Not on staff," I say. "But I know someone. Alexander Montgomery. He's on his own and kicking ass, but I think we can convince him to join forces. But he's going to want more than we want to give."

Reese tips back his glass. "Sounds like our man." He sets down his glass. "Let's talk to him."

"I'll make the call."

"In the meantime, does one of us need to go to Houston?"

"Now that I'm back to work, the storm seems to have calmed," I say. "If I have to go, I'll go. I'd rather wrap up the details on this case I've been dealing with, and weed through the new offers."

He studies me a few beats. "How are things?"

"You mean did I lose my fucking mind over Lori's attack? Yes. Am I dealing with it? Yes."

"Are you really? Because if Cat got attacked, I'm not sure how I'd react. It wouldn't be good. She'd most likely be tied to the bed where I'd keep her for the rest of her life, and happily, at that."

"I'm dealing with it, but Lori doesn't think I am."

"Why?" he asks.

"I turned down a case that was worth a lot of money."

"And she thought it was because you were afraid of putting her in danger."

"Exactly," I say.

"So is it her or you struggling with this?"

"She's so busy worrying about me that she can't face the part that involves her, which is why as much as I want to take her to Houston as I suggested and get out of here, I'm not sure that's a good idea. At some point, she's going to need to face this."

"She hasn't reacted to the attack at all?"

"She's been worried about me worrying," I say. "It's the damnedest thing."

"Marriage has a way of making you see the other person before you see yourself."

"Yes," I say. "It does." I narrow my eyes at him. "I just told you I turned down a case worth a shit-ton of money. You aren't going to ask why?"

"If I have to ask, you shouldn't be my partner, but if it was Carlson Wright, he called me next, and I turned him down, too. He's a low-life. Not our kind of client."

I laugh. "And that, my friend, is why I'm now in New York with my name on a wall next to yours. I need to finish wrapping up loose ends, work with the associates, and wait for a case I really want to win. That's when I win."

"As do I," he says. "Lori will learn that. She's a young attorney, but as a friend, let me say this: Maybe you should take Lori to Houston. See our new partner candidate. Get her away from the heat of it all and give her the room to melt down. Then come back and start fresh."

"Maybe," I say. "But Lori needs to feel in control. I'm not sure pulling her from the familiar does that for her."

"Right here, in this place, she *has* to have control," he says. "And that woman has worn a suit of armor for years. Maybe that means she really didn't let the attack get to her. Or maybe it means the effects are going to build and build under all that armor and explode without warning."

He's hit a nerve I didn't know existed, something bothering me that I couldn't identify. Under that armor, Lori was losing her mind when I met her, stressed and worried all the time. I'm supposed to be the person she can throw it away with. I'm supposed to be her safe place. My need to protect her has done just the opposite. I've forced her to put that armor back on.

Reese's phone buzzes with a text and he glances at it. "One of my associates. Let me call him and then we should go upstairs where our women await."

"Is Lori here?"

"For about ten minutes," he says. "Cat sent me a text when Lori was on her way up to give them about twenty minutes of girl time." He stands up and walks toward the bar.

Lori is here and didn't stop by and tell me. That doesn't feel right. I stand up, grab my briefcase and motion toward upstairs to Reese. I don't wait for him to join me. I need to see my wife. And if I have to, I'll take Reese's advice. I'll tie her to a bed and keep her there while I tear away that armor, inch by inch if that's what it takes.

Lori

I'm still standing in the bathroom, staring at the box that reads "pregnancy test" when Cat knocks on the door. "Well?"

I open it and hold up the box. "I haven't taken the test."

"Why?!"

"I don't know, Cat. I don't know. I just can't seem to make myself take it. Maybe that's why I haven't found a way to get the test. I'm afraid to find out."

Her hands come down on my arms. "Honey, this is not you. You aren't afraid of anything."

"Apparently I am. I don't know how I could worry over a baby when I just worried over my mother. And my father died and—"

"Deep breath. You are not pregnant, but if I'm wrong, and I'm not, you will be the best mother ever. Take the test."

"Cole and Reese will be here any minute."

"Reese is going to text me when they head up here. I'll warn you. Take the test. Should I stand here and supervise?"

"No, you will not," I say indignantly. "I'll take it."

"Hurry," she says, waving me back inside and shutting the door behind me. "If you hear the door," she calls out, "I'm expecting documents from the courthouse I ordered for my work-in-progress I want to show you. That means hurry, in case you didn't hear my first hurry."

"Right," I call out. "Hurry." I sit down on the toilet seat. *What is wrong with me?* I read the box. I've read it five times. It doesn't seem to matter. I read it two more times and then tear open the box. The test is officially in my hand. I set it on the sink, and press my hand to my forehead.

There is a knock on the door. I stuff the test back in the box. I'm doing this in the morning. It says morning on the box. My phone rings and I snatch it from my purse to find my mother calling. "Hey, mom."

"Why do you sound weird?"

"Because I was born that way?"

She laughs. "Ah, your father loved that joke. I miss him." She sighs. "I miss you, too. We're home. Can you and Cole come see us soon?"

"We'd like that. This weekend?"

"Perfect. And then I can thank Cole for that amazing trip to the Hamptons in person."

"Great. Yes. I can't wait to hear about it. I'll call you later this week. Are you back at work?"

"Tonight. I'm headed there now. Talk soon, honey."

We disconnect and there's a knock on the door. I stand up, determined now to move past this test tonight. I open the door and suck in a breath. Cole is standing there, big and broad, and perfectly male while holding a pregnancy test in his hand. "Why didn't you tell me?"

"There's nothing to tell. I didn't start my period, but the doctor said it's probably stress but I—I just—"

He drags me to him, his eyes dark, turbulent. Worried? I don't know. Maybe. "Are you pregnant?"

"I don't know. I can't seem to make myself take the test."

He kisses me. "Take the test."

"If I am—"

"Then you are. Then *we are*."

I nod, my heart squeezing with all kinds of unnamed emotions. "Okay. I need to do this alone."

"No."

"You aren't watching me pee on that strip, husband or not. You can help me watch after."

He nods. "Okay." He offers me the test.

I take it. "I have another one. This is a back-up."

He kisses me again. "Hurry."

"That's the word of the night," I say, my voice making this weird crackling sound. Like someone just pinched me or something. "I will." He shuts the door.

I grab the box and this time I just do it. I pee on the stupid stick. I cover it with a tissue because I can't look without Cole. I then wash my hands for a ridiculous amount of time and open the door. Cole's eyes meet mine, and I feel that familiar punch of awareness between us, but it's more now. It's this new level of intimacy and shared nervous energy. "How long?" he asks, shutting the door.

"It should be ready now," I say pointing at it.

"Why is it covered?"

"I didn't want to look without you."

"But you were going to take it without me?"

"No," I say. "I didn't. I was going to wait. And it says morning. It might not be accurate so even if it's negative, we have to do this all over in the morning."

"Take the tissue off of it," he orders softly.

"You do it."

154

He rubs the back of his neck. "Holy hell. Why are we hesitating?" He pulls me to him. "Whatever the result, I love you."

"I love you, too. Oh God. Just look."

He nods and we both turn and he pulls the tissue. We both stare down at it. "What am I looking at?" he asks.

I swallow hard. "Negative. No baby for us." My eyes burn and I cover my face.

He turns me to him, dragging my hands from my face. "What are you feeling?"

"I don't know. I think—I didn't want to be pregnant, but now that I'm not, I feel—let down. I don't know what I'm feeling."

"Me too," he says softly. "I feel the same. Like, it wouldn't have been a bad thing."

"It's the wrong time," I say, "and we never talked about this. We never—"

"I do. I do want us to have kids, Lori."

"You do?"

"Yes," he says brushing the hair from my eyes. "I do, but do you?"

"Apparently, I do. I hadn't thought of it and I feel afraid of what I could lose right now. You have to feel the same."

"Oddly, the moment I thought you were pregnant, that feeling faded. Like new life, somehow, heals the past, but like you said, this isn't our time."

"When is the right time?"

"We'll know. You'll know. When you're ready."

"When I'm ready?"

"You are still establishing your career. We're chasing your dream and we're going to enjoy every step of the way."

"And you're still establishing the firm."

"So, we wait. We enjoy each other, but if it happens by accident, let's not panic. Besides, we'll make beautiful babies together."

I smile. "We will, won't we?"

"Yes," he says, cupping my face. "And this is you and me. Together. Whatever happens."

"Together. Whatever happens."

"No one gets to take that from us. I promise."

CHAPTER SEVENTEEN

Lori

Cole and I exit the bathroom to find Cat and Reese at the kitchen island with a bottle of wine and four glasses they've already filled. Cat lifts the one meant for me. "Wine?" she asks, her way of finding out my test results.

"Yes," I say. "I would like some wine."

Cat winks. "Told you."

Cole reaches for his wine. "Why not wash two whiskeys down with wine."

"Exactly my thoughts tonight," Reese says. "And that's why God made car services. I also vote we order pizza, because I'm starving."

"My pastry butt is never going away," I declare.

Cole glances down at me. "Pastry butt?"

"I ate too much in Paris."

"But it was fun," he reminds me, his eyes warm.

"Yes," I agree, my cheeks flushing with the memory of him spanking me in that hotel room. "It was—*fun*."

He gives me a knowing look, his eyes burning hot. "We should do that again."

That.

Again.

He means he should spank me.

Reese clears his throat. "All right then. I'll order the pizza. I know what everyone likes by now."

Cole gives an evil laugh that has me nudging his leg in warning.

"And I," Cat says, saving us with a change of topic, "have something to tell you both. Your client connected with my publisher and I'm for sure writing his book. I'm going to make the world see the injustice served him and the heroes that his attorneys really are."

Cole sucks in a breath and downs his wine. "So we can get more attention."

"The book won't be out until next year sometime," she says. "And you know me. I won't publish anything you don't want published. I'll let you read it. Actually, I'd like you both to co-author with me. I think it will be brilliant, and there's a couple hundred thousand in it for you to split."

"And a press tour and attention we don't need," Cole says looking at me, and I can see his demons crawling out of the box. I can feel him pulling me close and trying to shelter me. "We don't need the money."

"We can donate our portion to the families," I say. "I can do the work with Cat. I think this book can expose the corruption of the legal system we want to be pure and fair. I want us to talk about it."

He studies me for several long beats in which I sense his struggle. I can almost feel him shove those demons back into the box. "You really want to do this?" he asks, proving despite his box of demons, he's still the man who helped me chase my dreams, who is always pushing me forward, not holding me back.

"I think I might," I say. "Cat and I are good together."

"We are," Cat says. "But no pressure. I just couldn't resist agreeing on that."

Cole looks between us. "You are. I know you are." He refocuses on me. "If you want to do it—"

"I want to talk about it," I say, kissing his cheek, and taking his hand. "With you. Later."

His eyes warm and before he can reply, Reese announces, "Pizza is on the way." He grabs the wine. "Let's move to the living room where we can talk about world domination."

Reese and Cat head out of the kitchen and I catch Cole's arm. "Any word from Walker on Ashley's ex?"

"Nothing," he says, snatching his phone. "I should text Royce." He punches in a message. "How was she?"

"Rattled," I say. "Really, how can she not be? Does she have family or anyone here?"

"She doesn't have anyone, period."

"Maybe we should invite her to stay with us?"

"Let's see what Royce says."

His phone buzzes with a return text. "No word yet," he says, reading the message and then sticking his phone into his pocket. "He's got calls out. They're watching Ashley. And he'll update me before bed. He's already communicated with Ashley."

"The flowers and the card were scary, considering he's supposed to be some sort of criminal."

"Maybe it was all a mix-up. It happens or we wouldn't have jobs."

The doorbell rings. "That will be Cat's delivery she was expecting from the courthouse. I should—"

Cole pulls me to him and kisses me. "What was that for?" I ask when I can finally breathe again.

"My way of telling you I'm here."

"You don't have to kiss me for me to know that, Cole Brooks."

"Then call it just because," he says, but it's not just because. It's something else. Something he wants to say, but is better said alone.

I suddenly want to leave, and hear everything on his mind and talk for hours if we need to talk for hours, but I like us as a couple with Cat and Reese. I like how normal and right that now feels. He does too, I see it in his eyes, but I think we both know that one of the best things we can do together right now is get back to a normal life. We need *normal*. We need things like pizza with Cat and Reese. I take his hand. "Let's go plan world domination," I say, laughing.

"Why are you laughing?" he asks, draping his arm around my shoulders as we start walking.

"*Because* I just had this mental dialogue about how good getting back to normal is, and then I said 'let's go plan world domination.'"

"Isn't that normal?" He laughs.

"Our normal," I say. "And I like it."

"Me too, sweetheart," he agrees, kissing me a moment before we head into the living room where the walls are windows, and the newly minted night sky is speckled with city lights. Reese is standing at one of those windows, and Cat is just returning from the door. "Another case that the DA let go," she says as we all sit down, me and Cole on a couch, while Reese grabs a chair, and Cat goes down on her jean-clad knees in front of the coffee table. "This paperwork is related to a case that proves the DA is all about the DA. An innocent man was charged and two more victims died before the DA finally looked for another suspect."

Cole leans forward, on alert now. "Sounds like you're launching a war against the DA."

"Someone needs to," Cat says, "but that's what I wanted to talk to everyone about tonight." The doorbell rings. "And that will be the pizza."

"I'll grab it," Reese says. "But hold that thought, Cat. I want to be a part of this conversation."

"How long ago was the case?" Cole asks.

"Two years ago," she says. "Someone the DA got off without any damage. No one sued. Not even the guy who was charged and put through hell."

"Sounds like a payoff to me," Cole says. "Have you looked for a money trail?"

"Not yet," Cat replies. "After writing the article about the DA mishandling your client, I got a tip on this from an anonymous source. I'm just digging in, but so far I think it's a legitimate story."

Reese returns with two large boxes and paper plates. "What did I miss?" he asks.

"I just told them about the tip I got," Cat says. "As for war, I want to take him down. He's supposed to protect people. He's not, but if I do take him down, I risk making the firm a target. He could come at every case you represent in ridiculously harsh ways."

I want to jump in and dismiss the risk. This has to happen, the DA has to go down, but this firm is Cole and Reese's blood and sweat. And so, I suck in air and I wait while Cat and I share a look of understanding. This is on our men to decide. It has to be, to be fair to them. Cole looks at Reese and they have a silent exchange that is short but intense before they share a nod. "We're doing this, then," Reese says. "Let's eat and talk about ruling the world that will be better minus a dirty DA."

I reach over and take Cole's hand and when he looks at me, I know my eyes are warm. He notices, his head tilting, a curious look in his eyes; a question I'll answer later when I assure him his demons are not winning. He is. He already won his own. *We won.* He just doesn't see it yet.

Cole

Normal.

That word stays with me the rest of the night while we visit with Cat and Reese. I want *normal, I want* to settle back in with Lori, but I don't want a version of normal where she feels she has to be the same super-human she was when she met me. I don't want a normal that includes that armor with me. And I did that to her with my box of fucking demons. In my need to protect her, I made her try to protect me. I'm going to fix that, and I'm going to start down that path tonight.

Well-fed and wined, we slip into the back of a hired car, and I pull her close, my hand on her leg. I never thought about kids until tonight, but with Lori, I want it all. Everything. Despite the punch in my chest when that test was negative, I'm grateful that she's not pregnant yet. We need to learn us first. We need to get past this one damn case that hasn't fully let us go, and travel a few more, just because we can. Because we're us.

We don't speak on the ride home, but the awareness between us is that palpable intense awareness I have known with no one but Lori. It's like a burn that slowly consumes, demands, even takes, but you give yourself to it willingly. And that's where I need Lori, where I almost had her, but she's pulled back, and neither of us even saw it happen. That's how much I was focused on how that attack affected me. What it made me feel when I was never what was important.

We arrive at the building and I help her exit, pulling her to me, my hands on her waist as I kiss her. "We're home. Our home."

"Yes," she whispers. "Our home."

I lace my fingers with hers and we start walking when my cellphone buzzes with a text. I fight the urge to throw the damn thing, but I snake it from my pocket and read the message from Royce while we cross the lobby. Once we're at the elevator, and actually, in the car, I stick my phone back into my pocket. "That was from Royce," I say, keying in our floor. "He says there's more to Ashley's ex than meets the eye. He might be CIA. He can't get a straight answer."

"CIA?" Lori asks incredulously. "That's unexpected. At least that means he's not dangerous."

"Royce said CIA doesn't mean he's not dirty or dangerous. We should hold for more information. We're not telling Ashley yet. He wants to wait. We'll know more in the morning." The elevator dings and we enter. "And now we're really home." I take her hand. "Come on." The minute I'm touching her again, the air is charged between us. I lead her down the hallway and once we're in the apartment, we leave our bags behind and I have her hand again, with one destination in mind: our bedroom.

We walk there in silence, and I know she can tell there is more on my mind than undressing. I guide her into the bedroom, but not to the bed. I walk us to the floor-to-ceiling window, and I pull her in front of me, the city lights dotting the inky sky. My hands cage her, and hers rest on the glass. I nuzzle her neck, inhale her scent, and I want to ask questions. I want to ask her how that attack made her feel. What she feels. What she fears. But I know Lori. She felt she had to be strong for me, and she built that damn wall again, that I had to have Reese jolt me into seeing that. The wall has to come down and without knowing it that first night when I spanked her, I had torn a piece of it down. I made her feel safe when she wouldn't normally feel safe. I have to make her vulnerable. I have to make her safe in that vulnerability and that means taking her someplace we haven't been. That means pushing her limits, tearing down her guard.

I sit down on the chair behind us. She turns to face me, leaning on the glass, a question in the silence between us that I answer with a soft command. "Undress, Lori."

CHAPTER EIGHTEEN

Cole

Lori is still standing in front of the window of our bedroom, the New York City lights speckling the night sky behind her. I'm still in the chair where I sat down, leaving her in front of me and with good reason. I need to be in control and not for me tonight, but for her. I've let my past make her feel she has to revert back to the days before she met me when the world was on her shoulders and there was no one to hold it up but her. I made her revert back to a place I never wanted her to be again. To a place where she didn't know I was there, holding it up for her. And so, we go back in time the way she has, and I remind her that from the day she met me she instinctively trusted me. She let me spank her. She let me be that person and place where she could just let go.

I remove my jacket and toss it aside, but Lori still hasn't moved. "Undress," I order again, as I had when I first sat down.

"You want me to undress?" Lori asks, a tentativeness to her words that isn't normally there, not with me. As if she senses what's in the air, as if she feels exposed and vulnerable when I'm the man who loves her, who would die for her.

"Yes," I say. "I want you to undress."

"You undress, too," she orders softly, but she doesn't move. She makes no attempt to undress when she's done it for me before, on the night we met, in fact.

"Not tonight," I say. "Not yet. I want to watch you."

"Why?"

"Because I do and because I want you to want me to."

She studies me for several long beats and then kicks off her shoes. Her jacket comes next. She tosses it on the chair on top of mine. "My blouse. You had to zip it this morning for me. I need you to unzip it now." We both know she can get it off herself and we both know that she's obviously trying to pull me back into the same space with her when I've set us apart for a reason. She expects me to stand up, to help her, but I don't.

"Come here," I order.

Obviously assuming she's won back control, she does as I say, but I don't touch her and I don't stand up. "Turn around."

She turns but still, I do not stand. "On your knees."

She rotates to face me. "On my knees?"

"Yes, sweetheart," I say, my hands going to her hips, offering her reassurance. "On your knees so I can get to the zipper."

"But you—"

"Stop asking questions. Do what I say and do it because you trust me."

Her eyes soften, an earnest look in their depths. "I do trust you, Cole."

"I know you do, but I think you've forgotten."

"I haven't," she says, her hands settling on mine. "Not even for a moment."

"Then turn back around and go down on your knees."

This time she doesn't hesitate. She turns and goes down on her knees in front of me. I reach out and brush her hair to one side and when I could unzip her blouse, I instead close my hands on her shoulders and press my lips to her neck. I want her to feel vulnerable, but I also want her to remember that this is me, this is us, and that means she can just let go. Just *be with me.*

She inhales with the touch of my lips, and lowers her chin, absorbing the touch, giving herself to the moment, and this pleases me. This tells me that wall is not wide or high, and just knowing this has me hot and hard, ready to pull her to me and make love to her, but that won't force her to pull that wall down. She's guarded herself with it for far too long. I reach up and drag the zipper of her blouse down to the middle of her back. Two of my fingers follow, gently gliding up and down her bare back. Goosebumps lift everywhere I touch, this reaction telling me she's one hundred percent right here with me, exactly where I want and need her.

The room is silent, complete utter silence, except for our breathing, and I let that encase us, let it consume us, let it tell us that there is only us here now. I slip my hands under her blouse and caress the silk off her shoulders. A soft sound escapes her lips and the barely there sound echoing through the room, heats my blood. I unhook her bra, and then she drags it all up and over her head, and when she would stand up, my hands settle on her shoulders, holding her in place. "Don't move until I tell you to move. Understand?"

"Yes," she whispers. "I understand."

I drag my hands down her shoulders, settling them for a moment at her slender waist before I'm traveling over her ribcage and cupping her breasts. She can't lean into me, not with her feet against the chair and that forces her to arch into my hands. I squeeze her roughly, my fingers closing over her nipples with no gentleness in my touch. She moans and covers my hands with hers, trying to turn, but I don't let her. That's not where this is going. I lean forward, widening my legs to press my cheek to hers, my hands settling back on her shoulders. "Stand up. Take off everything but don't turn around. Go down on your hands and knees."

"What?"

"You heard me. Repeat it. What are you going to do?"

"Turn around and undress you."

"Not tonight, sweetheart. Tonight, you're going to remind us both how much you trust me."

"Cole," she breathes out. "You know I trust you."

"Show me. Tell me what you're going to do and then do it. Now. Tell me now, Lori."

She pants out several breaths. "Stand up. Take off everything but don't turn around."

"And then what?"

"Go down on my hands and knees."

"Yes. Now do it and if you turn and face me, it ends. I'll go take a shower and we stop."

"Why would you do that?" she demands, obviously believing me, as she should. This isn't a night that I spank her for punishment.

"Tonight is all or nothing," I say. "We're all or nothing, Lori, and this is what we need tonight."

"You mean it's what you need?"

"No," I assure her. "It's what *we need*. It's what you think you don't need. *Trust me.*"

"I do," she whispers again and she moves, standing up and stepping toward the window. She stands there for a minute, no doubt, reminding herself of the vow she's just issued. She trusts me. No doubt convincing herself this is about me. She is doing it for me because Lori does almost everything for someone else, not herself, but this is very much about her.

She reaches for the zipper of her skirt, and slowly eases it down, sliding the material over her hips, and allowing it to pool at her feet. She kicks it away and reaches for the silk of her barely-there thong and holy fuck I want to go to her, to tear it away or just pull it down, but I do not. I watch her pull it down her hips until she is stepping out of it.

She's left in thigh highs and when she reaches for one of them, I say, "Leave them and you know what comes next."

"I turn around and undress you," she says, her voice raspy with a mix of nerves and arousal that pleases me. She's not thinking about anything but here, now, us.

"Another day," I say. "Another night. *Knees,* Lori."

She eases to her knees and when she would go down on her hands as well, I stop her. "Not yet. Stay just like that. Understand?"

"Yes, Cole, I understand."

I pull off my tie, remove my shirt and shoes but leave on my pants, which ensures I have an extra layer of control. I then grab the tie again and walk to stand above Lori, between her and the windows. She looks up at me, her beautiful eyes laced with anticipation. I kneel in front of her, my gaze raking over her naked body, her high breasts, and pebbled nipples. "Lace your fingers together."

She glances at the tie and then me, letting me see her understanding of what's about to happen and her agreement. She laces her fingers together in front of her. "I'm going to tie you up," I say, despite her silent agreement. "Any objection?"

"No," she says softly. "No objection."

I wrap the silk of the tie around her wrists and bind her. When I'm done, my hands settle on my knees. "Don't move. Don't turn." I search her face for agreement before I stand and walk into the closet and remove another tie from a drawer. I then kneel in front of a drawer, where I've placed a box filled with things I've wanted to share with Lori but have not. Not yet.

I return to the living room, set the box on the chair and then kneel behind her. For several seconds I just stay there, not touching her, my breath warm on her neck, until she gasps out, "Cole," and my name is a plea. To touch her. To fuck her. To end the blind torture, and yet it's just begun. I slip the second tie around her eyes and knot it into place. I lean into her then, press my cheek to her cheek and whisper, "Now I can do anything I want to you and you can't stop me."

CHAPTER NINETEEN

Cole

With Lori in front of me, her hands bound, eyes blindfolded, I repeat my words. "I can do anything to you, and you can't stop me." I slide my hand up her belly and cup her breast, a rough touch that promises I plan to push her.

"But I can stop you."

"How is that Lori?"

"I trust you. If I say no, you'll stop."

"Will I?" I challenge, tugging at her nipple.

"Yes," she pants out. "You will."

This is what I want from her: total trust. "Remember that." I run my hands up and down her body and she leans into me, exposed and vulnerable but fearless. She is with me. I'm holding her. This is safe for her, but it's not enough. Even bound, this is her safe zone and that doesn't tear down walls. I shackle her waist. "Hands on your knees and don't move."

I release her and ease back on my heels. She arches forward, grabbing her knees, more out of the shock of me no longer touching her than anything, I am certain. "Relax," I say, and it's a soft command, the kind I know she needs right now. It's not about being in control. It's about letting her let go of her control.

She inhales deeply but eases down into a full kneel in front of me, and her spine is straight, her hands on her knees. A submissive position that is all the more powerful because I know this woman submits to no one but me. I decide against the box, but I open it, grab a bottle of heated gel, and slide it under the chair. It's for later. It's too much right now, for this night. She's too guarded, we have too far to go, and knowing this kills me. I let her get here. I let us get here by allowing my past to control us.

Everything I might have done to her tonight shifts, changes, softens, but that doesn't mean I won't push her. I *will* tear down those damn walls. I will make her let herself feel what she's buried inside over her attack. I know what burying things rather than facing them does. I did it and that's why we're here now.

I squat behind her, touching her nowhere, but my hands caress an outline of her body. She tilts her head back and arches into the nonexistent touch as if she feels it; that's how connected I am to this woman and that's what I need her to remember tonight. Nothing she can feel or express or need is outside of my understanding. I reach up and just barely run my fingers over her shoulder, goosebumps lifting on her skin. I follow the touch with a true caress across that same stretch of creamy white skin, and down her upper arm. I repeat the same action on the other side. The barely there touch of her shoulder, the full caress down her arm.

A heavy, quivering breath escapes her lips, telling me how on edge she is, and I stroke the silky strands of her brown hair away from her delicate, slender neck, my hand on her naked shoulder, my lips at her ear. "I own you tonight." I brush my lips over her neck and then whisper in her ear. "And that means I'm going to push you and push you some more." My lips trail down her neck to her shoulder, where my teeth scrape before my tongue soothes that bite.

She yelps and I lave the offended skin with my tongue. "I promise to make it hurt really good."

"I don't like being tied up," she whispers.

I reach around her and pull her back against my chest, my hands cupping her breasts, fingers teasing her nipples.

She moans and I lower my head to ask. "What don't you like?"

"I want to touch you."

"I want you to touch me, but not yet." I lean around her and kiss her, her lips and tongue reaching for mine, the taste of her hungry and yet uncertain. Desperate and yet reserved. It's the unknown that is consuming her right along with me.

I squeeze her breasts. "Lean forward on your hands and knees." My hands fall away from her.

"Are you going to—"

"Spank you?"

"Yes," she says.

"You might like that a little too much to make it a surprise." I smack her backside. "On your hands and knees."

She yelps with what is a surprise, arching against my touch, but she pants out a breath and does as I command, her palms flattening in front of her, her perfect backside lifted high in the air. Her hands and knees are on the soft thick brown rug that I'm damn glad I let the decorator talk me into buying. I stand up and undress, just the sight of her on her hands and knees, thickening my already hard cock. I wrap my hand around it, a momentary memory of her on her knees in the shower, her mouth on me, almost my undoing. I want to drive inside her, to fuck her, and start all over, but no. That's isn't what I'm going to do.

I settle on one knee beside her, pressing my hand between her shoulder blades, and leaning into my hand on her lower back and slender belly. "On your elbows."

She complies, and I drag my hand down her spine to rest on her backside while my lips press between her shoulder blades. "What are your limits, Lori?" I ask, my teeth scraping her shoulder again.

"I don't know."

"Let's find out."

"What are you going to do?" she asks urgently.

"Make you forget everything but me." I press my hand to her belly.

"Success," she whispers. "I'm already—"

The fingers of one of my hands brush her nipples, while the other traces the line down the center of her beautiful bottom. She never finishes her sentence and that's how I want her. Speechless, mindless. I squeeze one of her breasts and then the other, tweaking her nipples, only to abandon them and move behind her, flattening a palm on her lower back, my other hand sliding up and down the center of her backside, stopping just over her sex, the wet heat of her arousal radiating over my palm. I know what she likes, I know what she wants. I give her a slight smack there, not meant to cause any pain, just pleasure. This delivers her earthy, wanting gasp and I can hear her breathing now.

I grab the gel and pour it on my hands, pressing my palm to her sex, and sliding the liquid over her. She whispers my name and I slide a finger along her sex front and back, dragging all the wet heat up and down her entire body, lingering in that intimate part of her I have never dared. "Cole," she whispers, panic in her voice. "Cole, I—"

"Easy, sweetheart. Only pleasure. I won't hurt you."

"I know. I just. I—"

My fingers press inside her sex. She pants and I sink them deep and spank her at the same time. She arches into the touch, and I do it again, pulling my fingers back and thrusting them inside her at the same moment I spank her. "Sink to the ground," I order.

She does it almost on instinct and the minute she's on the floor, I roll her to her side and then to her back, spreading her legs and sinking between them. I waste no time giving us both what we want. My mouth closes down on her clit, suckling, licking, stroking. She moans low and deep, sexy as hell. Her knees shackle my shoulders, telling me how on edge she is, how in need. I respond. I give her more, my fingers pressing along her sex, but this time when I enter her, I penetrate her front and back. She goes stiff but a few strokes of my tongue and she eases into the sensations. I'm gentle where I need to be gentle, placing all intensity on her sex with my fingers and my tongue and she quakes into a sudden, intense orgasm.

I bring her down, and when her legs stop trembling, I untie her hands, and slide up her body, tearing away the blindfold, my pulsing thick erection setting between her legs. My eyes meet hers and the heat and intimacy between us is scorching, the trust there is a new level of trust, and we need no words. I press inside her, watching her lashes lower as I stretch her, fill her. "This is where I want to be the rest of my life," I tell her. "And this is how I want to taste." Her lips part and I claim her mouth, kissing her, the taste of her on my tongue now on hers. It's a slow kiss, a passionate kiss, and our bodies begin to sway and pump.

We make love until we snap and suddenly we're fucking, me driving into her, her legs at my hips, while hers lift into every drive of my cock. The need for this woman is everything, consuming me, and when her sex clenches around me, I'm helpless in a way no one else can make me. I'm shuddering into release while her body quakes around me. I lose all time, and holy hell, it's fucking beautiful; she's beautiful, and when we melt into the sated, perfect moment after orgasm, I hold her. Just hold her. That is until I hear her sob. I pull back to look at her.

"It's not you," she whispers. "I promise you, it's nothing you did. I don't know why I'm crying."

But I do. It's like that first time I spanked her when she cried. The adrenaline rush, the fear of the unknown releases endorphins, and the high became a crash, a release of pent-up emotions. I roll us, and pull her to me, under my arm, ready to ride out the storm with her. This is what I wanted. For her to just let go, and when she let go, the walls fall, and she faces what's on the other side.

She was attacked.

But as she sobs, deep gut-wrenching sobs, her entire body trembling, I think this is more. She's finally crying over everything she has faced; losing her father, almost losing her mother, her struggles to survive. And so, I hold her even closer, and ride out the storm with her. The way a man should ride out every storm with his woman, *his wife*. Thankful she finally let me in, thankful she's finally letting everything else out.

CHAPTER TWENTY

Cole

I hold Lori through the storm of her tears and when she finally calms, she doesn't move. For several minutes, she seems to just melt against me, but she isn't asleep. I can feel her thinking, and I give her room to breathe, the way she did for me when I was the one dealing with my demons. I stroke her hair, and she presses her hand to her forehead and sits up. "I don't know what that was." She rolls away from me and grabs my shirt, pulling it around herself.

"I'll be right back," she says, but I catch her hand and sit up, kissing her.

"You okay?"

Her hand settles on my jaw. "After I pee I will be," she says, offering me a tiny smile. "A girl has to go when a girl has to go." She tries to pull away, but I catch her fingers and kiss them.

"Hurry back."

"I will," she whispers, the humor of moments before gone. She stands up and rushes away.

I stand up and walk into the closet and pull on a pair of pajama bottoms before I pursue Lori, finding the bathroom door shut. I inhale and remind myself to give her space, but after ten minutes, I knock. "You okay in there?"

She opens the door, her dark hair wild from my fingers, but her tears are gone, her smudged make-up with them. "Yes. I'm okay."

I reach out and snag her fingers. "Come talk to me," I say, walking backward until I know she's agreed.

She nods and I lead her back to that lounge-style chair, seating us side by side, staring out at the inky skyline twinkling with a mix of stars and city lights. "I don't know what that was," she whispers.

"Everything," I say. "That was everything finally happening."

She looks over at me. "It was, wasn't it?"

I reach over and stroke a piece of hair from her eyes. "Yes. You needed that. I want you to know that you the strongest person I know, but with me, you let down your guard. And I won't ever betray that, I'll never hurt you. I'm not ever going to let you down. I'm not ever going to judge you. I'm never going to think because you admit what you feel, or need me, that you are weak or a different person."

"I don't know if I even know how to do that. The way I've dealt with the hard stuff in life is just to make it go away. Charge forward. Don't look back."

"You mean, like me, you shove it all in a box, and then that box pops open without your permission, like mine did. Give it permission, and let's deal with it. What are those things in your box?"

"My father. What my father did to us still eats me alive. It affected me with you at first, but you're you. It doesn't anymore."

"Are you sure about that? Because after your attack, you pulled that wall back up."

"I didn't."

"You did," I say. "And that's my fault. I had my struggles and you did what you do. You stand strong for everyone else. Let's both try standing together to be strong."

"We do," she whispers. "Cole, I have never felt so complete with someone, as I do with you."

"As I do you, Lori, but that doesn't mean that years of fears and conditioning just go away. We have to work at this. I know I do, and I am. I told you about my mother. I haven't told that story to anyone else."

"I am not holding back."

"And yet you haven't reacted to your attack, not until tonight."

"The attack—I just put it in that box, but I don't remember making that decision. There were other things to face. Other things to worry about."

"You mean me."

"What's wrong with that?"

"It's in the box, Lori. It's going to come out."

"It's not. If I'm honest, it made me feel out of control, so I dealt with it. I shoved it aside, but I wasn't hurt or raped or anything like that. It's solidly buried."

"Lori," I begin but she leans forward and kisses me.

"If it does come back," she says, crawling onto my lap, straddling me, her hands on my face, "I'll tell you right away. I promise, but you have to give me room to breathe. When you're nervous, I get nervous, too. When you hold on so tightly, I feel like I need a shield. I don't know how we balance this out."

"Together," I say. "We need to talk like this. We need to do it together."

"Together," she whispers, and I decide I've cracked that wall, even if I haven't fully lifted it, while she's reminded me that I have to control my demons that I know are feeding hers.

I unbutton my shirt that she's still wearing, sliding my hand up her back, molding her to me. "I'll be here. I'm not going anywhere." Our lips collide and this time we make love, passionate, gentle, but no less fierce. We kiss, we touch, we repeat and when I enter her, her body rocking with mine, I feel her right there with me, all of her. I'm going to make damn sure it stays that way.

Morning comes too early considering I want to keep Lori in bed, but after showering together, her light mood and eagerness to dive into work, hunt down a new case, and get us back into the swing of things, is contagious. We've stopped in a coffee shop, waiting on our order when she turns to me, her glossy pink lips inviting me to kiss them. "About that book Cat wants us to write," she says.

Now I just want to take her home, fuck her, and make her forget that damn book and this case that has become hell. Instead, I say, "You really want to do it, don't you?"

"Yes," she confirms. "You say I buried my attack. Maybe you're right, but this book about this case, our case, won't let me. It makes me, and us, face the attack and get beyond it. I think it's good for both of us, but I know this affects us both, so I won't move forward if you're wholly against it."

I resist my need to just get her, and us, the hell away from a trial that lead us to so damn much torment, but she's right. This keeps her, and us, from burying something in a box that will later come back and haunt us. "Do it then," I say. "I'll help where you need me, but you and Cat write the book."

She gives me a beaming smile, pushes to her toes and kisses me. "I'm excited about doing this. Cat and I are good together. She brought me to you."

"Well then," I say, my hand molding her closer, "I owe Cat a thank you I haven't given her."

We arrive at the office to find Ashley sitting at her desk, the flowers she'd received from her ex nowhere in sight.

"What happened to your flowers?" Lori asks.

"I had them delivered to a retirement community who won't see a bastard when they look at them."

Ouch, I think, when Lori softens her voice and leans on Ashley's desk. "How are you?"

"I have Smith as my hot bodyguard," she says, her voice strained. "How can I not be fine?" She glances at me. "Thank you for that by the way."

"No thanks needed," I say. "I'm always happy to supply my assistant with a *hot bodyguard*."

That earns a tiny laugh from her and a bigger one from Lori, but everyone sobers quickly. "We'll get answers today," I promise.

"You have about ten prospective clients to deal with," she says. "You don't have time for me and this." She holds up a file. "I put together notes on all of them."

Lori accepts the file and glances at me. "I'll do this." She looks between us and then focuses on Ashley. "Then Cole can help you." She doesn't wait for an answer, but rather glances at me. "I'm going to my office. I'll let you know if there's anything important to deal with." She takes off, and I try really damn hard not to watch her leave, but she's in that damn pink dress that hugs her backside just right.

Forcing my attention back to Ashley, I get back on task. "I need to speak to Alexander Montgomery. Hunt him down for me, will you?"

"Alexander Montgomery? Are you working a case with him?"

"More like a business proposal and you can tell him that." I soften my voice. "We'll handle this," I say, and then head to my office.

I've just settled behind my desk when Royce calls. "The FBI wants to talk to Ashley. I'll sit in and host the meeting here at my office."

"The FBI," I repeat. "I thought this guy she was engaged to was potentially CIA?"

"They're sharing limited facts right now, but I've pressed to ensure Ashley's safety and I feel they are responsive to my pressure more than anything."

"I'm going to need to sit in," I say. "I don't want her pulled down in some criminal investigation like she was in Paris."

"Understandable," he says. "The meeting is at six. Do you want to talk to Ashley or me?"

"I will," I say grimly, not looking forward to this talk. "We'll be there." I disconnect and buzz Ashley. "I need you."

"Of course you need me," she replies, trying to be her flippant self, but it's a choked attempt that tells me how stressed she really is.

She enters my office and I motion to the door. She shuts it and crosses to stand in front of me, her black dress as dark as I suspect her mood to be. "What's wrong?" she asks, sitting primly on the edge of her chair.

"Royce found out that your ex may be CIA."

"CIA?" she breathes out. "Really?"

"Really."

She makes a frustrated sound. "I want this to somehow make him less of an asshole, but he didn't tell me. I was still some token in a game. Clearly, I still am."

"I don't know how to respond to that other than to remind you that we don't have facts. The FBI wants to interview you tonight. I'll sit in and so will Royce Walker. It will be at his office."

"Is that a good or bad thing?"

I repeat what Royce said. "He's working to protect you. Let's assume that's what this is."

"But I need you," she says flatly.

"Of course you need me," I say, giving her a wink.

She swallows hard and gets up. "I need to go work and get my mind off of this." She walks to the door and I call after her.

"You aren't alone," I promise, and she hesitates with her hand on the knob but doesn't turn. A few beats pass and she says, "Thank you," and leaves.

In the wake of her departure, I think of how alone Lori was when I met her despite having her mother. How alone I was before I met Lori. And Ashley is exactly that: Alone. No family. No one but us. It makes a man really appreciate his wife. It makes a man want to get up, find his wife, grab her and take her on a desk somewhere. I'm about to stand up with the intent of finding my wife and doing exactly that when she peeks her head in my office.

When she sees that I'm not on the phone, she enters my office and shuts the door. "There's a case I want to talk about."

"Bring it to me," I order softly, scooting my chair back. "Here."

CHAPTER TWENTY-ONE

Cole

The minute my door is shut and Lori has joined me on this side of the desk, I back her against the desk, my hands on her hips. "What are you doing?" She laughs as my fingers slide down her hips toward her hemline.

"Finding out what color of panties you have on," I say, walking her skirt up her thighs.

She grabs my hands. "No," she says firmly. "You wait until tonight."

"Just let me look."

"No," she chides, holding up the file in her hand. "Murder case. Really interesting. Please read it, but I'm warning you. It's a federal judge's wife. It's going to get lots of attention, but we have to take it. I *want* to take it."

"If I read the file—"

"You'll make me very happy," she supplies.

"Well then," I say. "I guess I better read it." I accept the file and set it on the desk before updating her on Ashley.

"She must be a wreck," Lori says. "I'm going to see if I can take her to lunch. Maybe talking will help her."

"Order in," I say, sharper than I intend. "I don't want you out with her."

"Cole," she says, her hand settling on my shoulder. "I thought you were easing up."

"This isn't about a case, Lori. I'm paying for security for Ashley for a reason. The FBI is involved for a reason."

"Right," she concedes. "You're right. We'll order in. I almost overreacted. I'm sorry."

I kiss her hand. "Just protecting what is mine and you are *mine*."

"Yes," she says, cupping my face. "I am." She kisses me. "I'm going to ask Ashley to lunch, in my office." She smiles and heads toward the door, peeking over her shoulder to say, "Those pink panties you like so much."

I groan, and she laughs, shutting me in my office, alone. I'm about to reach for the phone when my eyes settle on the file she gave me now laying on my desk, I know it's a fight ready to happen. I open it and start reading and confirm my assessment. Federal judges lead to politics, this particular one especially, and there's nothing more volatile than politics which isn't necessarily something the firm needs in its newly formed identity.

I have to hope Lori understands this, but my gut says that she'll think I'm holding back to protect her, that I'm incapable of giving her the freedom I know she craves and the growth she deserves. If I'm not careful, that's exactly what will happen, and that would be my mistake again. I can't insist that Lori tear down her walls while I try to hold her captive, but deep in my gut, I still feel what I felt right before we returned from Paris. Trouble hasn't finished with us yet.

Lori

Ashley and I sit down for a lunch that includes salads and soup, which suits my intention of losing my five pounds quite well. "How are you feeling about everything?" I ask, then add, "Though we don't have to talk about this if you don't want to."

"It's fine. It really is. I'm fine. I have to be, right?" She jabs her fork at her salad before continuing, "How do you love someone that was a lie? That makes the love a lie, too."

"But it didn't feel like a lie," I surmise.

"No." She swallows hard. "It felt more real than anything I've ever known." She shuts her eyes. "I'm not sure how I was that foolish."

I have no idea why but I get the sense that despite her reactions, she wants to talk. "How did you meet him?"

"Jogging and texting. I ran right into him, as in literally. Of all the men I chose this tall, dark, and gorgeous man to run into. I thought it was a fairy tale. And now, I think it was a set-up. I was an easy target. I don't have any family. If I disappear, no one misses me."

"Is that what the authorities told you?"

"They thought I was an accomplice."

"To what?"

"I never got that answer. It's crazy, right? Not to know what I was accused of? But I was in another country and I heard the word 'spy' several times. Spies don't get the same rights."

"You think he was a spy?"

"I have no idea, Lori. I'm being guarded from a man I was going to marry. I'm clearly not objective."

"What can I do?"

"Listening helps. Thank you."

"Of course. Do you want me to go to the FBI interview tonight?"

"No," she says. "I wish Cole wasn't going. I'd like to learn what kind of fool I am on my own, but I know that would be foolish."

"Call me after, will you?"

"Yes. Of course."

"Maybe you should make out with Smith. It might make you feel better."

"I wish it would," she whispers, no laughter in her voice.

We finish up lunch, and Cat and I finally end an all-day game of phone tag. "I'm in for the book! When do we start?"

"Yay!" she says. "Tonight. How about the coffee shop around six?"

"Six it is."

We disconnect and I smile. Things happen for a reason. I left school and that lead to Cat and Cole. I wonder where this all leads for Ashley? I wish it were to her Cole. I trust Cole and she trusted this man, too. Maybe she trusted him just as much as I do Cole. I'd be crushed if Cole wasn't what he seemed. *Shocked.* Destroyed. Any way you lose the person you love destroys you.

Savage brings an SUV to the office to pick up Cole and Ashley for the meeting, and I hitch a ride to the coffee shop. I don't miss the fact that Savage, who is normally quite the personality, is silent. "Good luck, everyone," I say, hugging Ashley before Cole steps out of the car to help me exit, offering me his hand.

Once I'm on my feet, he pulls me close, kisses me, and in a short stroke of his tongue, he has curled my toes and managed to make me moan. "I'll come back and get you."

"Savage is weird. Did you notice?"

"Yes. He never keeps his mouth shut and his mouth is shut. I'll find out."

"Make the FBI tell you what's going on," I say. "If anyone can, you can." I kiss his cheek and head into the coffee shop, but I feel Cole watching me. When I step to the door, I turn and wave to him, and only then does he get in the car. He's still getting used to our normal again and since I'm a little antsy, maybe I am, too. Not maybe. Those tears last night showed I am affected by the attack. I don't like it, but it's true. It just drove home that there are too many things in life, like death, that we cannot control.

I find Cat at our normal table, and it feels like old times. I hurry across the coffee shop and the two of us are quickly in deep conversation. "I didn't think Cole was going to go for this," she says. "He's very protective."

"He's getting over it. It was pretty intense. Roger was running at me and he's big while it was a small space." I think of Cole's mother, of the little boy watching his mother's attack, and my gut twists. Certain Cat will read more into my silence and ask questions, I stand up. "Let me go order coffee." I rush to the counter and order, texting Cole: *Good luck. Love you.*

He doesn't reply, which means he must already be in the interview. I sit back down waiting on my order, and Cat and I start plotting. I try to focus, but I just keep thinking about last night. Cole holding me. Me crying. I don't know why this is happening right now while I'm with Cat. I'm obviously on edge. It's Ashley. I'm worried about Ashley. She has no control. I know what that feels like. It's like hanging on a ledge by your fingers that are bleeding, barely breathing as you do. I should have gone with them to the meeting.

Cole

I'm back in the SUV with Ashley beside me, but I'm still thinking about Lori. I have no idea why I had to force myself to let her go into that coffee shop without me, but I did. I promised myself I wouldn't let my demons suffocate her. "How close is the interview location?" Ashley asks beside me.

"Ten minutes," Savage says from the front seat. "The agents are already at the office, looking all Men in Black or Matrix. Yeah, Matrix. They have on glasses."

"Wonderful," Ashley says. "Now all I need is the Terminator waiting on me."

Savage gives a bark of laughter. "Good one," but even then, he's stiff. Maybe it's personal. Maybe he knows something I don't know.

We finally arrive at the Walker offices, and Smith is waiting to escort Ashley inside. I fall back to talk to Savage. "What don't I know?"

"One of the agents is an ex-friend of Royce's. It's like having two caged tigers inside who want to rip each other's throats out. Great fun, if Ashley wasn't in the middle of it."

"Wonderful," I say, steeling myself for war. "Let's go do this." I head for the door.

I walk inside and Royce greets me. "Ashley is in the conference room. The agents are in an office. They sent someone I consider a bastard ex-friend. This meeting is not to help Ashley. You need to protect her, while I have someone in the CIA try to get me real answers. I don't know what Ashley's ex-fiancé is or was, except trouble. Prep Ashley and let me know when you're ready. And make sure there's nothing she hasn't told you." He leads me down the hallway and he's about to open the conference room door when his phone buzzes with a text. "Houston, we have a problem. Roger is free. They let him go."

"The man who attacked my wife?"

"Yes. Him."

"How soon?"

"Already done. An hour ago."

And now I know why I didn't want to leave Lori at the coffee shop. My demons were winning. I felt this. I felt *him.* He was there. "Get someone to her. Get me to her." I pull my phone out and dial Lori, but she doesn't answer. I run for the door.

CHAPTER TWENTY-TWO

$\mathcal{L}$ori

Cat and I are digging into the list of people we want to interview for the book when I realize I've finished my coffee in about fifteen minutes. I hold up my empty cup. "Guess what? Empty and I can't think until I go to the bathroom."

Cat laughs. "Want another? I'm going to grab one. I can get you one."

"Yes, please." I'm already standing. "Can you watch my purse?"

"Your phone is ringing," she yells as I head for the bathroom.

"I'll call whoever it is back!" I call out, certain it's not Cole since he's in the interview, and my bladder will not wait. I reach the door I'm seeking to find it locked. Great. Just great. I eye the men's room. I might have to use it. A man passes me and enters, stealing that great idea right out of reach. I am dying. I knock despite the fact that I hate when people do that, but I'm desperate here. Another full minute passes and finally, the woman in the bathroom exits with her lipstick freshly polished, which she clearly did while I suffered.

I quickly enter the bathroom, lock myself inside and do what I need to do. Sixty seconds later, I am a new person and I wash up, glancing in the mirror while flashing back to last night with Cole. He pushed me hard. I grab the sink, a rush of so many memories filling my mind. Cole touching me, kissing me, taking me, and us, places that we have never been, but I know it wasn't about the physical. It was about trust.

Cole doubts my trust, but he's wrong to do so; I trust him. I hate that he feels otherwise and all because when I feel unsettled, or out of control, I immediately insulate myself. I know I do. I needed to be there for him, so I blocked out everything that might make me weak, including my attack. I don't know how Cole would have dealt with my attack, though, if I'd been weak, if I'd crumbled. I did the right thing. I was strong for him, but deep down I know I'm still guarded, still afraid of being hurt, or loving Cole so much that I can't live without him and then I have to. I need to just talk to Cole. I love that man. He listens. We'll figure it out. And that certainty is why I shouldn't be afraid. I know him. I know us. He is a part of me.

I suddenly remember the phone call and the idea that it might be my mother and she might need something hits me, though of course, she has her new man. She's fine. Everything is fine. I breathe. I'm not running out of here in a panic to call my mother. I need to deep breathe. I need to stop expecting the worst. I can. Will. Because of Cole. I'm stronger with him than without him and I don't say that enough. I'm going to tonight.

I open the door and gasp. A tall, bulky man who is all too familiar is standing directly in front of me, as if he was pushed up to the door, waiting for it to open. Shock radiates through me. "Roger," I gasp t and back up. "What are you doing here? How are you here?"

He stalks toward me, forcing me further into the bathroom, and when he's able, he seals us inside. "I only shut the door so I can talk to you without someone stopping me." He holds up his hands. "I mean you no harm." His eyes are bloodshot, pained. "I don't know who I was the day I came at you. I didn't mean to scare you."

Anger rushes over me and so many pent-up feelings. I'm shaking all over. "You didn't mean to scare me? You ran at me. You trapped me. You punched my husband."

His face reddens. "I thought you were—I thought you got off a killer. Her killer. My sister's killer." He runs fingers through his hair. "I lost my mind. I've never done anything like that." He leans against the door. "We lost our parents in a car accident. I was a teenager, sixteen. She was twelve. I dragged her out of the car and—" He looks away and then back at me, tears streaming down his cheeks. "The car exploded. My parents died. Our parents died. I've always protected her." His lashes lower, torment ripping over his features, seeming to gut him and it's then that I realize that I'm crying with him, shaking with the impact of his emotions slamming into me. He looks at me. "I didn't protect her this time. I thought you didn't either, but you did. You and the people around you are why he's in jail now."

"This wasn't your fault," I say. "You aren't the reason she died. He is. He's a monster."

"I was supposed to take her to dinner that night. I had a woman I'd been asking out finally agree to have coffee with me. I cancelled on my sister." His fists ball at his sides. "I fucking cancelled dinner."

Oh my God. I feel punched. I don't know how to help him, but I want to. I need to. "It's not your fault."

"Stop saying that. I wanted to scare you. I wanted to scare your husband. I wanted to make you pay. I don't deserve your sympathy. Just—I'm sorry. I won't ever bother you again."

He opens the door and exits and I follow him, gasping as Savage shoves him against a wall. "Cuff the bastard," he shouts at Smith.

"No!" I shout. "No. No! He was apologizing."

Savage looks at me. "By cornering you in a bathroom. I don't think so."

"Please," I say. "He just—he's—"

"Lori!"

At the sound of Cole's voice, I rotate to have him grab me, pulling me to him. "Tell me you're okay. *Tell me.*" He pulls back to look at me. "Lori—"

"I'm okay, but he was just apologizing. Please make them uncuff him."

"No. No, I'm not making them uncuff him. I can't. He violated his restraining order."

"He's in pain. He said—he said so much." I start crying again. "Please. I can't let him get taken away." I turn in Cole's arms to find Savage shoving Roger out the back door. I press my hands to my face, and tears burn through me.

"Lori!"

At the sound of Cat's voice, I just can't turn. I'm too tormented by that man's pain and the idea that I've just added to it. She steps in front of me and hugs me. "He pulled her from a car before it exploded," I whisper. "And watched his parents die in the car."

She pulls back and Cole must have heard because I feel his hand tighten on my waist where they've settled. "Oh God," she whispers, tears springing to her eyes.

"He was supposed to have dinner with her that night and he cancelled for a date."

"Oh my God," she says, again. "That poor man."

Savage opens the door and shouts, "This way."

I rotate in Cole's arms. "We have to help him. Please."

He cups my face. "There are many ways to help him," he says. "But everything you just said only makes me fear his instability. We have to be careful."

"I know, but—" I cover my face again and my knees wobble.

Cole scoops me up and starts carrying me toward the backdoor. Not more than sixty seconds later, I'm in the backseat of an SUV with him, and no one else in the vehicle. "You weren't there," I say, rotating to face him. "You didn't see his face."

"Exactly," he says. "I'm objective."

"I'm your wife," I say, grabbing his lapels. "You're not objective."

"There is not a man on the Walker team that believes he doesn't need a further psych evaluation. He was failed, and not by us. He needs help. We'll get that for him." He strokes my cheek. "Protecting you comes first. Think if it was reversed."

I catch his hand. "I know. It just—it was powerful, Cole. You heard what I told Cat?"

"I heard, sweetheart."

"What happens now?"

"The police will want to talk to you and we could put it off, but if we want him back in a hospital, I think we need to do it tonight. If you're up to it."

"Yes. Tonight. I am. I'm fine. He didn't hurt me. He scared me and then he just gutted me emotionally. Let's talk to the police."

Hours later, Reese, Cat, and her brother, our attorney, Reid, have all joined us at our apartment and we sit around the living room. Cole has me plastered to his side like he's afraid Roger will come snatch me away. I'm pretty okay with that, though. My walls—gone. My defenses—gone. Tonight, I'm just going to lean on my husband.

"How did this even happen?" Reese demands, standing up to pace in front of the window.

"A paperwork issue," Cole explains. "They let him out without informing us."

"My ass," Reese says. "The DA is behind this."

"He's pissed about the lawsuit," Cole concedes, "but a revenge act would be foolish. What if Lori had been hurt?"

"But he would have been told Roger was cleared and safe," Cat interjects. "Maybe he thought he'd spook us when we found out Roger was free and we didn't know."

"And it backfired," Reese says, looking at Cole. "He knows we're investigating him. This was a threat that went further than he expected. I'd bet my right arm on it."

"I'll be paying him a visit in the morning," Reid says, speaking for the first time, eyeing Cole. "Care to join me?"

"I'll be there before you," Cole says.

"I'll be there as well," Reese adds.

"I want to go," I say.

"No," Cole declines quickly, turning to me.

"Yes," I say. "I might be shaken, I admit that, but never have I been better ammunition for that man's defeat."

He studies me several long moments and then looks at the rest of the room. "I need to be alone with my wife."

They all agree quickly, and Cat and Reese hug me. Reid gives me a stoic nod. They head to the door and Cole follows them. I grab the blanket on the couch and wrap it around me, walking to the floor-to-ceiling window wrapping the room to press my hand on the cool glass, stars twinkling in the dark sky, tiny lights in the darkness. The way Cole was my light in the darkness, but Roger has no light. He's been cut and cut again, bleeding rivers, and I felt like I was drowning in them tonight.

I feel, rather than hear, Cole approach. He steps behind me, pressing his hands next to mine on the glass, his big, hard body a shelter I welcome. "You scared the hell out of me tonight," he whispers by my ear.

I rotate to face him. "Please tell me you aren't going to fight me about going to the DA's office. I need to do this. I need to not only do this, but I need to be the best at my job I can be. I need to learn from you and do more. I need to make a difference."

He studies me for several long moments, his expression hard then softening. "I'm not going to fight you."

"You aren't?"

"No, but there is much I want to say and do to you tonight. For me and you. To remind us both we're here, and we're staying here, present, together. For fucking ever." He tangles fingers in my hair. "You want to deal with this by fighting back. I do, too." His mouth closes down on mine, in a passionate, burning kiss I feel in every part of me, and then he is picking me up and carrying me toward the bedroom.

CHAPTER TWENTY-THREE

Cole

I carry Lori into the bedroom and set her down on the bed, and as much as I'd like to make love to her, now is not that time. We need to talk and she needs to come down from tonight's high, not be taken on another one. "Are you hungry?" I ask, standing in front of her.

"Actually yes. Starving."

"How about Chinese?" I suggest.

"I'd love that, but can we hold off for a few?" she asks. "I just want to sit in a hot bath and get my thoughts together."

I stroke her cheek. "Of course. I'll give you some space to unwind. We can talk over dinner."

She catches my hand and kisses it before her eyes go wide. "Oh, God. Is this on the news? Will my mother hear about it and freak out? I don't want her stressed. I never

213

LISA RENEE JONES

even told her about Roger. We had it so hush-hush and she was in the Hamptons at the time. Now, what if it's not?"

"I'll call her to be sure and reassure her you're fine. If she seems worried, you can call her after your bath."

Her body softens, tension easing from her muscles. "Thank you, Cole."

"Go take your bath." I step back to allow her room to get up and she pushes to her toes, kisses my cheek and heads off.

I turn and watch her enter the bathroom, amazed at how strong she is. I'd really believed that she was hiding from a meltdown over Roger, but I'm not so sure anymore. Sure, she cried tonight, but over his pain, not her fear, and her response to all of this was—she has to do more. That's what she needs and realizing this helps me shove my own demons back in the box. I cannot love a woman and keep her by my side as I want to for the rest of my life if I suffocate her, if I keep her from her version of more.

I walk down the stairs, forcing myself to give her space. She deserves time to process what she feels, not what I feel. Once I'm well out of her hearing range, I dial Reid. "Any updates on anything?" I ask as he's promised to make phone calls and get to the bottom of the mess.

"Still working on it and I have a stockholders' meeting for a takeover I just managed in the morning. I'll come to your office when I'm done."

"Any idea when?" I ask, sitting down on the coffee table.

"After lunch. And that's a better option anyway. We all need cool heads and more information before we make our next move. I would have told you that earlier, but I didn't want to set Lori off in any way."

"Right," I say. "You're right. Call me when you head our direction."

"Will do," he confirms and disconnects. I immediately dial Royce Walker. "Where is Roger now?"

"In jail," he says. "He was evaluated. They declared him sane. He violated the restraining order."

I press fingers to the bridge of my nose. "Who's his attorney?"

"Marks. Donovan Marks. Do you know him?"

"I do not. Do you have his number?"

"I'll text it to you, but I need to know your plan here."

"Happy wife, happy life," I say.

He laughs. "Don't I know it."

"Which is why," I continue, "I'm going to find out how to protect her and help Roger. I need to know if he gets out,

215

even if I have to pay your team to sit at the jail around the clock this time."

"We'll handle it," he assures me. "I hate to bring this up, but the FBI still wants that interview with Ashley and soon."

"It needs to be Wednesday. I need to deal with Roger and the DA tomorrow."

"I'll set it up," he says. "Same time and place?"

"Yes. That works. Where is Ashley?"

"Smith took her home."

We disconnect and I text Ashley: *We're home. We're safe. We rescheduled your interview for Wednesday night. Are you okay?*

She replies instantly: *Yes. And thank God all is well. Just take care of Lori. I'll see you tomorrow.*

My phone buzzes with a text. I hit the number to auto-dial it and the man I assume to be Donovan Marks answers. "Marks."

"This is Cole Brooks."

"I won't ask how you got my number. My client apologized to your wife. He meant her no harm."

"While my wife believes that," I concede, "I'm not as forgiving. I saw what he was like the day he attacked her and it was brutal. Get him to accept a mandatory ninety-day hospital confinement and I'll drop the charges."

"The hospital assures us he's stable."

"How many stable people have you seen commit violent acts? Because my list is long."

"He will have financial concerns," he replies, sidestepping a direct answer.

"Bigger ones when I put my best foot forward and lock him away for a few hard years."

He's silent for several beats. "I'll talk to him."

"You now have my number." I disconnect, hoping like hell I've solved the Roger problem.

With my wife on my mind, I walk into the kitchen, pour her a glass of wine and head up the stairs. I find her neck deep in bubbles, her hair piled on top of her head. "How's the bath?" I ask, closing the space between us, and setting the wine down on the ledge surrounding the tub.

"Heaven," she says. "I already feel better. I swear I had this chill that just went to the bone." She reaches for the wine. "Thank you." She sips. "I know you have updates on Roger. Tell me."

I sit on the ledge. "He's in jail."

She sets the glass down on the other side of the tub. "I knew he would be. I hate that he is. I truly believe that man just lost his mind with grief."

LISA RENEE JONES

"You aren't remembering his face and eyes in that bathroom," I say. "You can't or you'd know he's not someone we can dismiss."

"But Cole—"

"Hear me out. I am giving him the chance to get help. I called his attorney, but I'm going to create layers in this deal to protect you. And all of this when I really want him behind bars. I can't want to help a man I believe would have hurt you. I'm not made that way, but I love you. And I'm doing it this way for you."

She softens. "Thank you, Cole."

I squat down next to her. "How are you? Not how do you think you need to be. How are you?"

"I'm okay, but I get this need to do something when I feel out of control. I need—"

"To do more."

"Yes. We aren't even really looking at cases right now. I *need* a case. Honestly, I think you do, too."

She's right and yet I feel the resistance inside me. This fear that I'm still digging us out of one hole and we'll land in another.

"Let me order the food and we can talk."

"That feels like resistance."

"It feels like hunger to me and I just realized that I have not yet called your mother." I kiss her cheek and grab my phone, walking into the bedroom and ordering the food, before dialing her mother.

"Cole," she greets. "Is something wrong?"

"Nothing is wrong."

"Then why are you calling me?"

"Lori and I had a run-in with a man that has caused us trouble as it relates to a case. It's handled. No one was hurt, but she was afraid it would get on the news and be blown up."

"If she's okay, why isn't she calling me?"

I walk to the bathroom. "She's chin deep in bubbles in the tub." I hold out the phone. "Shout a hello to your mother."

"Hi, mom! I'm fine. I have bubbles and wine and Cole."

And Cole.

God, I love this woman. I wink at her and place the phone back at my ear. "See. All is well."

"Except she let you call me because we both know she's more upset than she is letting on. You do know that, right?"

"I know she has her way of dealing with things," I say. "We both have to give her room to do that."

"Right. You're right. You *do* know my girl. I want more details."

"We'll come see you this weekend," I say.

"Sooner would be better, but I'll accept that." She pauses. "Hug her for me?"

"I will." We say our goodbyes and I peak my head back in the bathroom. "I told her—"

"We'd come see her this weekend." Her eyes soften. "I heard."

My phone rings and I glance at the number. "Reese," I tell her. "I'm sure he's just checking on you. And I ordered the food ten minutes ago now." I depart the bathroom and head back downstairs.

"Reid just sent me a text about tomorrow afternoon. I'm in court."

"I'll handle it and I'm still trying to reach Alexander Montgomery for the Houston changing of the guard. I'm going to try to get him here to us, so you can meet him no later than the weekend. If I can't I'm staying case-free until I lock this and Houston down fully." We chat for a few minutes and when we disconnect I think of Lori's need to take a case. She's ready on her own. It's me that has to get fucking ready to let her be on her own. The doorbell rings, and I grab the food.

A few minutes later, Lori and I are on the bed, eating and talking. "You're still not ready to take a case," she says, returning to that hot topic.

"We're bringing in a Houston partner. I need to handle that before I take on anything high-profile, outside of managing the associates' cases."

"But you left Houston to run the company here. Why bring in a partner?"

"Houston needs a fresh start to be a valuable asset, not a potential liability."

"What about sending Ashley there? Can you at least keep an eye on things?"

"When she gets past this problem with the FBI and her ex, maybe. And that interview is now Wednesday, by the way." I set my plate aside. "I'm going to need to go there and I'd like you to go with me. Then you will know the lay of the land if you ever need to step in."

Her brow furrows. "You'd trust me to step in?"

"You might not be a seasoned lawyer, but you are loyal and smart, as well as my wife."

"I will do whatever I need to do to support this firm." She studies me a moment. "I *need* a case."

"I do know that. I'm not trying to hold you back. *I won't* hold you back." I lean over and kiss her. "If the perfect case comes in, one that one or both of us are passionate about, you or me or both of us, will take it. I promise. Deal?"

"You say that but I feel the hesitation in you. I know you are trying to get a grip on your need to protect me and after tonight, it's got to be rekindled. But after tonight, I need to say something to you." She sets her food aside. "That wall you say I have?"

"You admit you have a wall?"

"Not consciously, but I was thinking about that on the ride over here and in the tub. I do have ways of protecting myself."

"Like my mental box, I shoved the past in."

"Yes. Pushing you away at first was part of that. That kept you from being able to hurt me like my father hurt me and my mother. I pushed everyone away but Cat, and she's the reason I found you." She waves that off. "The point is that if I stay away from the courtroom for much longer, I fear that Roger cripples me. I need to get back on the proverbial bicycle. When I said I need to do more, I meant *I need* to do more and I think you do too. We need to just do it. Take a case. Get past this. Stop letting it control us. We need to do that now."

She's opened that shut door. She's really talked to me about her fears. She's allowed herself to be completely vulnerable and what's more, she's right and so I say that. I pull her to me. "Yes. We both need this. It's time to take another case and win."

CHAPTER TWENTY-FOUR

Cole

I wake with Lori in my arms and mentally issue a vow to keep her here and safe, but I also warn myself that holding on too tightly will destroy her and us. I don't just love this woman. I admire her strength and what I saw in her last night was not fear of Roger, but fear of losing herself to fear itself. And so, I set aside everything but waking up with this woman, sharing a life, and of course, her picking out my light blue silk tie for the day to match the pinstripe in my gray suit. I pick a red dress for her, because a) her ass is perfect in it and b) I don't plan to suffocate her and hide her. The dress is bold like I hope she will feel again, soon. She knows this instantly, I am certain, as the choice earns me a kiss and a smile.

I head downstairs before Lori to receive a call from Royce. "Roger tried to kill himself with a sheet last night. He's being sent back to the hospital."

My jaw hardens. "In other words, I'm a shitty person for feeling relief right now."

"You're human. He was unstable and he now can't get to your wife. More later." He disconnects and Lori joins me.

"That was about Roger, wasn't it?" she asks stepping in front of me.

My hands come down on her shoulders. "He tried to commit suicide, but he's alive and being moved to the hospital again."

She inhales a breath and lets it out. "Let's go to work and find that case to take."

"Yes, let's."

We arrive at the office early and Lori is quick to make coffee and huddle up with Ashley. Reese is quick to check on Lori and I update him on what I know thus far. After which, Lori takes residence in my office at the conference table with a stack of files, determined to find our case while I deal with two junior attorneys and a case gone wrong. In other words, I'm going to court this afternoon, and that means Reid will have to wait until I get back.

When the junior associates leave my office, my phone buzzes. "Alexander Montgomery on the line," Ashley says.

"Are you finally going to tell me what this business proposal is?"

"Why do you ask so many questions?" I ask, not ready to mention the word "partner" to her when that change may not even happen. And change makes people uneasy, even if it's a good change. She doesn't need more uneasiness right now.

"It makes me good at my job. I know all. I see all."

"Put him through," I say, motioning for Lori to shut the door.

"Cole Brooks," he says. "You've been busy, winning cases and moving. I had no fucking clue you'd left Houston."

"Bullshit, Alex. You were glad I left and gave you a chance to get the good cases."

"And yet, you're calling me now," he says. "I must be good for something."

"I want you to come here and talk about a business proposition," I say.

"Give me more than that. I have a trial starting in a week."

I fill him in. "I'm possibly intrigued," he says when I'm done. "Honestly, man, until I get through this case—"

"There will always be another case. Fly in. Meet Reese. Talk to us. This weekend. Hell, we'll prep for your case over dinner."

His pen taps on his desk in a steady five beats before he says, "Let me see what I can work out. I'll call you late tonight."

We disconnect and Lori gives me a hopeful look. "That sounded promising."

"It's an open door," I say, texting Reese with an update. I stand up. "I'm going to check on where the prep for court stands."

"I'll be here," she says. "I put a call into that judge I told you about. I want to set a meeting for you to talk to him about his case."

Tension radiates through my body at the mention of the case I'd hoped she'd let go. I walk to her and pull her to her feet, my hands on her shoulders. "This case is not our case."

"Because it's too high-profile and you don't want another Roger," she says flatly.

"Because I'm being smart as a managing partner of a newly merged firm. It's a political case and that means the firm is assumed to be political. That means there won't be one Roger, but many. And they won't be coming after just you and me but everyone here. We cannot do that, go after the DA, and manage a crisis of management in Houston."

She inhales and lets it out. "Right." She softens and presses her hand to my jaw. "I understand. Completely and I was shortsighted on this."

I kiss her hand. "Not shortsighted. Excited about what you do. It's important to choose cases that you feel passionate about, but there is more than excitement and even guilt and innocence to consider."

"A lesson learned." She kisses me. "Go do your job. I will continue my hunt for the perfect case."

Relieved, I exit the office as Royce sends me a text: *Can you talk? Alone.*

Not liking how that sounds, I dial him immediately. "What's happening?"

"My brother hacked the hospital records, which stated that the restraining order was cancelled. No notification was needed."

"Which isn't true."

"Which means the paperwork was tampered with. This DA is powerful and dangerous. He must know that he's being investigated and that didn't come from my team."

"Reese's wife has been digging around," I state.

"She needs to stop and you need to convince the DA there is a truce in the making. Get on his good side. You don't go at a man like this full frontal. Let my team do their jobs."

"I'll talk to them," I say. "What else?"

"More soon."

We disconnect and I walk straight to Reese's office, motion to his door, and his secretary confirms he's alone. I enter and shut the door. "The paperwork was changed on Roger's discharge papers. Royce Walker thinks the DA is behind it."

"Good. Lori is safe and we can use this to take him down."

"He wants us to back off. He seems to believe the DA is dangerous. He believes the DA knows we're coming for him and Royce wants us to make a truce with him and let him set the asshole up. Pull Cat back."

He tosses his pen on the desk. "That's like pulling a tornado back that's already spiraling, but yeah. I'll pull her back. What else?"

"More soon."

He nods and I exit the office, and holy hell, I'd invite a good case to dig into right now. Lori is right. We need a case and we need one now.

It's nearly seven when Lori and I join Cat and Reese at their apartment. We're gathered around their island finishing off a pizza waiting on Reid and Royce for a plan when Royce shows up. He claims the endcap. "We have leads on some low, dirty actions by this DA that don't just border on criminal, they *are* criminal. We need some space to pull together damaging evidence but he'll cover it up as long as he feels watched. He's now on guard. We need to back-up, give him space, and act slowly but precisely."

My cellphone buzzes with a call from Reid and I let him know who is in the room before I put him on speaker. "Look all," he says. "I have a company takeover in process. I can't stop by, but here's what you need to know. One of the board members of this company I'm managing somehow got word that I'm suing the DA. He's tight with him. He let me know he is not pleased."

"And you're pulling out," Lori assumes.

"Hell no," he says. "I'm not pulling out. Sorry, ladies, but I told him to go fuck himself and I'd buy him out. He acted like I stuck something up his ass when I didn't get the pleasure and then went on his merry way. I'm in. I'm going after the bastard, but I'm damn glad circumstances didn't allow you all to charge into his office with me. I'll get you your settlement, but this board member suggested you're going after the DA on a bigger level. I need to know what I'm into and not on the phone."

"I'll come see you tomorrow," Royce says. "Where?"

"I'll text you the address. Call me directly to coordinate."

"Will do," Royce says and when I disconnect the line, he adds, "Let Reid go at the DA on this lawsuit, and then it's over. Back away."

"Make nice when they're suing him?" Cat asks. "Is that possible with this man?"

"I can do it," Lori says, and we all look at her.

"What does that even mean?" I ask.

"I'll play the victim who needs his help, of course," she says. "I'll tell him this case has touched my heart but scared me too, and I just need it behind me. I'll plead with him for a way to do that and praise his record."

"If he knows we're going after him," Cat says, "that won't work."

"It will if I tell him how much those close to me have freaked out, and how I'm pulling them back, too. I need everyone to just put this behind us. I'll make him believe that for my sanity, everyone has agreed. I'll do it right. I'll cry. I'll convince him. I'll even offer to do a press conference with him."

"I do not want you putting yourself on the line with this man," I say. "No. Absolutely not."

"Actually," Royce says. "It might protect her and everyone else in this room. Why would he reject a press conference and positive press when he wants reelection?"

Lori turns to me and grabs my arms. "I'll close him. I can do this."

I look skyward and force myself to be reasonable. She's right. Royce is right. "I'll go with you. He needs to hear from me that I'm backing off."

"No," she says. "I'll close. I'm not his adversary. You are. I can do this. I need to do this alone."

CHAPTER TWENTY-FIVE

Cole

She wants to go to see the DA on her own.

That's not going to happen, but I'm not having that battle with my wife at Cat and Reese's house, with them standing across the island from us and Royce Walker staring at us. I focus on him now. "If we back out of this, we need to know you're really bringing this man down."

"A DA looking out for himself and hurting innocent people in the process is not someone that sits well with my team. All of my people have, and do, risk their lives to save innocent people. He's devious, but I have people on my team that have taken down warlords that would make that man cry. We'll get him, but the idea here is to do it without him taking down you and your team first."

"That would be a plan I approve of," Reese says, glancing at Cat. "Keep the book you're writing about the murders that started this off the grid."

"Whatever you need," Royce says. "Tell me."

"I'd like to go to North Carolina where the real killer was arrested and interview people down there," Cat says. "Is there any reason I can't do that?"

"As long as you focus on the killer and the process of catching him and leave this DA out of the picture," Royce says, "you should be fine."

Cat glances at Lori. "Want to go to North Carolina with me?"

"After I know Ashley is safe," Lori says. "If she ends up in some sort of witness protection, Cole will need me here."

Cole will need me here, I repeat in my mind. I always fucking need her, and the closer the better, which is just another reason she and I need to talk about the DA.

"Is that where this is headed?" Lori asks, directing her attention to Royce. "To Ashley landing in witness protection?"

"I can't answer that question," he replies. "Not because I don't want to or have been silenced, but because the Feds aren't talking right now. They want to hear her story first. And yes, they said that."

"Do they think she's guilty of something?" Cat asks.

"My read is that they think she knows something they need to know," he says. "That doesn't spell guilt. She may

DIRTY RICH CINDERELLA STORY: EVER AFTER

not even know she knows it. Or maybe she does and she's protecting him."

"I don't get that read," Lori says. "She's angry, hurt and confused."

"I'll talk to her tomorrow," I say. "I'll make sure she's not holding back, under client-attorney privilege, which I'll formalize."

Royce's phone buzzes with a text message and he glances at it and us. "I need to run, but let me return to the DA for a moment. I believe Reid Maxwell can be an asset. The financial backers behind this DA are at the root of his power. Reid manages the kind of corporate power that can make or break a man. I'm going to be talking with him in detail."

"As am I," I say. "I've told Reid to go at this DA for the settlement. On that, I won't waver. This is for the families of the victims. And while we'll assure the DA we're backing off otherwise, the lawsuit is staying in place."

Everyone agrees and once Royce departs, I waste no time saying our goodbyes. Even then, it's far too long before Lori and I settle into the back of a hired car to take us home. *Home.* My home is with this woman. That's damn surreal. I pull Lori close to me, my hand on her thigh, just beneath the hem of her skirt. It's only then that I allow what I'm really feeling to surface and take hold. I'm angry.

Lori should not have insisted on going alone to see the DA without talking to me.

She covers it with her own and glances over at me. The minute her eyes meet mine, the flicker of a street light illuminates my face and she narrows her gaze on me. "You're angry."

"We need to talk. We'll probably fight." I lower my voice. "Fight and fuck, remember? We never said we wouldn't."

"Right," she says tightly and tries to move away.

I hold her steady. "You're moving away in anticipation of the fight that hasn't happened?"

"I'm warming up for battle."

"Is that right?"

"Yes. That's right."

I cup her face and whisper. "I'll warm you up." I lean in and kiss her, my tongue doing a slow slide that has her panting into my mouth.

"That's unfair," she whispers, eyeing the driver.

I scoot us further behind the seat, and kiss her again, my hand sliding up her skirt to her panties, where I brush my fingers. She grabs my arm and mouths, "No," right as I shove aside her panties and drag my finger along the slick seam of her body, pressing two fingers inside her.

"Cole, damn it," she hisses, as the driver calls out, "We're here," and the damn car pulls to our building.

I force myself to remove my fingers, tugging her skirt down, and pressing my cheek to her cheek, my lips by her ear. "Let's go fuck the fight out of our system."

I open the door and offer her my hand. She stares up at me, glowering with the promise I will be punished, which can only mean a little shouting and a lot of fucking. That works for me. She declines my hand and exits the car. I pull her to me, kissing her before my arm wraps around her shoulders and I tip the driver. We walk into the building and Lori doesn't try to pull away, but I can feel her anger just as readily as I can feel her need. We enter the elevator and we are not alone. Not one but, a group of six join us, and I step to the back of the car, pulling Lori in front of me, settling her backside to my hips, the thick pulse of my erection pressed to her backside. My hands at her waist, inching upward, my thumbs stroking the sides of her breasts.

She catches my hands and tries to turn, but I hold her firmly in place. We arrive on our floor with the car still packed. The minute I release her, she dashes forward. I snag her hand from behind, ensuring she doesn't escape through the crush of bodies. Once we're outside the car, I fold our arms at the elbows and put us in motion toward the door.

We don't speak and she doesn't pull away but she's going to. The minute she gets the chance, if she starts to dart away, or tries, I'll catch her. We reach the door and I pull her in front of me, my body holding hers in place. I stick the key in the lock, and I turn it. Lori opens the door and rushes inside. I grab the key, lock the door, and pursue. She's already disappeared around the corner. I peel away my jacket and then I'm on the hunt.

I catch up with her just in time to find her entering the kitchen, putting the island between me and her. "Sex isn't getting you out of this," she promises. "We fight and fuck. The fight comes first."

"Tonight we fuck, fight, fuck." I move toward her.

She moves away. "No, Cole."

"Yes, Lori."

She darts around the counter and once again, I'm on the opposite side of her. "You know I'm going to grab you, and undress you, and fuck you, right? That's happening."

"You don't want me to talk to the DA alone. I am. That's happening."

"Let's negotiate naked."

"The only way I'm negotiating naked with you is on my knees with you halfway to completion."

I laugh. "Is that right?"

"Yes."

"I can live with that. Come over here."

"No."

I arch a brow. "What happened to you on your knees and me halfway to completion?"

"I'm going to see the DA alone."

I round the counter and this time when she tries to escape, I don't let her. I snag her hand and pull her to me, trapping her between me and the island. "Talk first," she says, her hands on my chest.

"Sorry, sweetheart, but I've already been between your legs in that car. Talk after."

"No."

"Yes." I turn her to face the island and drag her jacket off her shoulders, but when I would remove it, I tangle it around her arms, and then turn her to face me again. "You were saying?"

"This changes nothing. I need to convince the DA—"

I lean in and kiss her, a deep stroke of tongue before I say, "Nothing you say to the DA will matter if I don't convince him I'm pussy-whipped and doing what you want."

She laughs. "Like anyone would believe that."

"Sweetheart, anyone that's with us five minutes knows I'll do anything for you." I reach up and rip the buttons off her shirt.

She gasps, and I swallow it with my mouth over hers before I repeat my words, "I would do anything for you."

"Then let me go alone."

"As long as I get to storm in and convince him you went on your own and then negotiate that settlement."

"That's your plan?"

"Yes."

"Oh."

I pull her bra down and tweak her nipples. "Do we agree?"

"Yes," she agrees.

"Then either you're going on top of the counter with your legs on my shoulders or you can go down on your knees and make me promise."

"I have no hands."

"Your point?"

She bites her lip and says, "I want that promise." She goes down on her knees.

CHAPTER TWENTY-SIX

Lori

I wake pressed close to Cole and smile. This is my life now. I start every day with this man holding me. This is not someone else's fairy tale. It's mine and it's real. "Morning," Cole murmurs, kissing my forehead. "You're awake."

I raise to my elbow to look at him, a light stubble of dark brown shadowing his jaw, his hair a rumpled, sexy mess. "And you're wide awake."

"Not for long."

"You're worried about the DA," I say.

"No. I woke up holding my wife, and decided to enjoy it before the alarm went off."

His cellphone rings on the nightstand. "Or my phone rang. And so, it's already begun." He reaches across me, kisses me hard and fast in the process, and then grabs his phone to glance at the screen. "Reid. I'll put him on speaker." Cole punches the answer button.

"What the fuck, Cole?"

"I guess you got my message," he says, dryly pushing to a sitting position to rest against the headboard.

"You want to go at the DA on the morning I tell you I have a stockholder meeting for an important project? No. You wait."

"Good morning, sunshine," I say, sitting against the headboard next to Cole.

"Sunshine, my ass," Reid snaps. "You wait, Lori. We do this when it's time and it's not. I've left the DA squirming for a reason. I want him to come to me. I want him to wonder why I haven't taken a piece of his ass. I'm close to getting you four times the deal you wanted. He cannot believe that you're willing to back off. Not yet. You want to make nice with him, you do it after I finish making him suck his damn thumb."

"I take it you want us to wait," Cole says dryly.

"Finally, one of you gets the point," Reid says.

"I'm daring to challenge you on this," I say. "I think if I go in there and tell him how much I just want this over, how much I want to make peace, he'll be more likely to settle."

He's silent a few moments. "I'll think about it. After my meeting. Don't screw this up in the meantime." He hangs up. Cole and I look at each other.

"I think we need to do this sooner than later, before the DA makes a move that burns the firm."

"Agreed, but an extra day won't matter," he says. "Let's give Reid room to breathe so that he can focus and talk objectively about our next move."

My cellphone rings now. I grab it to find my mother. "Hey, mom," I answer quickly. "Is everything okay?"

"Of course. I'm at work and I knew you'd be getting up to start your day. I just wanted to see if you're okay. You haven't called me since your attack."

"I'll make coffee," Cole whispers, standing up in all of his naked glory before he pulls on his pajama bottoms and heads for the door.

"It wasn't an attack, mom. He was grieving for his sister—it's complicated. I got emotional because I felt his pain. That's all."

"I see. I'm sure you did. Can you help him?"

My stomach knots. "He tried to kill himself. He's okay though and I can only hope that the good in this is that it helps ensure he gets real help."

"I suddenly really need to see my daughter. I know you're very busy but can you and Reid do dinner with your mom and her very special man?"

Her very special man. I still can't get used to her with anyone but my father and yet, after the way my father left her to struggle, she deserves happiness. "When?"

"Whenever you can. I'm off Thursday, Saturday, and Sunday but we can always go to breakfast if needed."

"Let me talk to Cole and I'll let you know our schedule so we can coordinate with yours, but I'm looking forward to it."

"I want you to come to our place. I want you to see how good this man is to me."

I swallow hard. "Yes. I'd like that."

We say our goodbyes and disconnect right when Cole walks into the bedroom with two mugs. "Why are you frowning?"

"My mother wants us to come see her new home and how well her man takes care of her."

He sits down and hands me a cup. "Again. Why are you frowning?"

"I shouldn't be. I want her to be happy, but..."

"It's stirring up feelings about your father."

"Yes. They were in love. I do know this. In the end, he wasn't all he should have been to her, but they were in love. I suddenly feel sad that my father is just forgotten when a few months ago, that's what I wanted."

"Maybe, just maybe, this means you're starting to forgive your father for his mistakes. Therefore, he's human again, not a monster who betrayed you."

I sip my coffee and consider this. "Do I want to forgive him, Cole? He gambled. He left us in debt. He left us desperate as my mother had a stroke."

Cole sets his cup down and then mine. "Yes. You do. He was not perfect, but you have always told me that until the end you believed you were loved. Gambling, like drinking, is an addiction. He needed help."

"Are you ever going to try to forgive your father?"

"Never. He was," he considers a moment, "like the DA. He didn't have a problem. He was the problem. He was just a monster." He looks skyward and then settles his hands on my arms. "I'm not him. I will never be him. I promise you, Lori. I will always love you, protect you, and put you first."

I'm not sure if he's saying this for me because of how my father makes me feel, or for him, because of how his father makes him feel. Actually, I do. He's saying it for us.

Everything is for us now.

Cole

Lori and I walk to the coffee shop, and we're waiting for our order when Roger's attorney calls. "Under the circumstances," he says. "My client agrees to six months in hospital treatment in exchange for you dropping the charges."

"Good. Put it in writing."

Lori grabs our coffees and hands me mine, waiting eagerly for news, which I share. "It feels like this is almost over, doesn't it?" she asks, as we exit to the street.

"It feels like we're getting there," I agree.

"Now we just need a new case," she says as we arrive at the office, and step onto the elevator a good forty minutes early.

I glance over at her. "Yes. We do." And I find I really mean that. We're ready. I'm ready.

She rewards me with a beautiful smile and it's a smile that I want to see for the rest of my life.

We enter the executive offices to find Ashley already at her desk, hard at work. I watch her interact with Lori and it's clear to me that she's not good. She's not feisty and snarky. Her eyes are bloodshot with dark circles beneath them. Even her dress is black, like she's in mourning. Lori notices, too, giving me a look that we both understand. I need to talk to her. Lori heads to her office, and I eye

Ashley. "Grab a dollar bill or whatever you have and come to my office."

She frowns and reaches for her purse. I enter my office and grab the contract I did up for Ashley before I left the house this morning. She joins me and I motion to the conference table where we sit across from one another. She holds up the dollar. "What is this for?"

"Hand it to me."

She does so and I push the contract in front of her. "Sign that."

She scans it and looks at me. "Free services?"

"Of course, free services. Sign."

She signs and offers it back to me. "Thank you, Cole."

"Thank me by talking to me."

"What do I say, Cole? The man I loved lied to me and now the FBI wants to talk to me."

"What haven't you told me?"

"Nothing."

"What haven't you told me?" I repeat.

"*Nothing*. That's what hurts. I believed he was who he said he was."

"Which was what?"

"Retired military. Contract security consulting, which is why he traveled a lot. You know this. I told you."

"And yet I never met him."

"Because he traveled so much."

"They think you know something you aren't saying," I say.

"Who? The FBI?"

"Yes."

"Oh God. They're going to try to take me down with him, aren't they? And if he's CIA, that has to mean he's some sort of spy. That's what was talked about in France." She stands up. "They think I'm a spy."

I stand up with her. "You're okay. You've got me, remember? I'm good at what I do and I'm less concerned about them using you for bait, and more concerned about them pushing you into witness protection."

"What? You think—I don't want to go into witness protection. They can't make me, right?"

"No. They can't make you, but if you think—"

"No. I mean—Oh God. I need to go home. What if I'm putting the people here in danger?"

"If they felt that, they'd already have you in protection."

"Then why even suggest they will later?"

I hold up my hands. "It's my job to prepare you for any possibility."

My phone buzzes. "Alex is on the line," the receptionist announces, "and Ashley isn't answering her phone."

"I'll take it," I say. "Give me thirty seconds and put it through."

"I need to get to my desk," Ashley says, trying to pass me.

I catch her arms. "It will be okay, but I need you to think hard about anything you know that I need to know before tomorrow's meeting."

"Okay," she says, but she cuts her gaze and pulls away, walking toward the door. She leaves and shuts me inside and I curse. There's something she isn't telling me.

My phone starts to ring and I head to my desk, grabbing the line. "Alex. Give me good news."

"I'll fly in Saturday, but I need to leave Sunday morning."

We make arrangements and I buzz Reese and let him know the plans, but my mind is still on Ashley and that meeting with the FBI. I dial Royce. "Reid had us hold off on making nice with the DA."

"He told me."

"Good. Moving on to why I really called. I'm concerned Ashley is keeping secrets and I have no good reason that she would do that. She has attorney-client privilege."

"I've done my research," Royce says. "I have nothing to offer. Whatever she's hiding is buried."

"But the FBI could know what it is and we don't," I say.

"They could, yes. It's unlikely or they'd have handled this interview more aggressively, but it's possible."

"Dig deeper."

"When she was stuck in France, we did. There is nothing to find."

We talk for a few minutes and disconnect, my fingers thrumming on the desk. Ashley said herself that she could be dangerous. She's my assistant that I brought into this firm. I have a responsibility to protect everyone here. I dial Royce again. "You want to push the meeting up to tonight," he assumes.

"Yes. Now that the DA confrontation has been delayed, I need to know what this is and if it's dangerous."

"Understood."

"I want Smith to take her home until the meeting and stay with her around the clock."

"Also understood. I don't blame you. We'll bring her here. She can hang out in our building. We're one hundred percent secure. I'll send Smith to you now."

We disconnect and I cannot get this FBI meeting done soon enough.

CHAPTER TWENTY-SEVEN

Cole

The minute I hang up with Royce, I exit my office and walk to Ashley's desk, kneeling beside her. "Royce and I just talked. He's going to take you to his offices where we know you're safe until we find out what is going on with the FBI."

She squeezes her eyes shut and looks at me. "You mean where you know I can't be a risk to everyone else. I get it." She opens her drawer and grabs her purse. "I'm ready. I assume I have an escort?" She stands up and I follow her to her feet.

"Smith is going to take you, but Ashley—"

"Don't explain. You're being smart. I should have considered this."

It's at that moment that Smith, a tall, broad man with sandy brown hair, heads in our direction. He's dressed in jeans, a T-shirt, and wears a thin leather jacket. "He has a gun on under that jacket," she says, glancing at me. "That should comfort me. It's doesn't."

"We're going to get through this. Royce is moving the meeting up to tonight. We'll get answers."

"Tonight?" Her voice quakes.

"Yes. Tonight."

She looks away. "Okay."

Smith stops beside us. "Ready, Ashley?"

"What girl isn't ready for a hot guy with a gun?" she asks flippantly, but her voice cracks.

He gives her a direct look. "Then you know everything is just fine." He offers her his arm. "Come on."

"I don't need your arm. I'm fine." She walks ahead of him and he and I share a look.

"She'll be okay," he promises before quickly pursuing her.

Lori passes them and stops in front of me. "What just happened?"

I pull her to me and kiss her. "I'll explain in my office, and if I could take you home right now and take you to bed, where we would stay all day, I would. We need a day like that. Just you and me." I lace her fingers with mine and pull her into the office.

A few minutes later, we're both sitting on the couch and I've just updated her on the situation. "Maybe I should talk to her," she says. "I'll go over to Walker Security."

"I don't want the FBI thinking you know something that makes you a problem."

"But you can know?"

"I'm her attorney."

"I'm your co-counsel." She takes my hand. "Let me talk to her. I'm a woman. I'm the closest thing to a friend here she has."

My cellphone rings and I pull it from my pocket. "Royce," I answer. "What do you have for me?"

"The FBI can do five o'clock. Can you?"

"Yes. We can. I'll be there at three." I glance at Lori and reluctantly add, "Lori wants to come over and try to get her to talk."

"She has a connection with Smith. I told him she needs to talk to us before the FBI. Let him try to work his magic."

"I'll tell Lori." I disconnect.

"You'll tell me what?"

"There's a little bit of a connection between her and Smith, which I sensed as well when he just picked her up. Royce is having him talk to her. Let's see how that goes."

"I don't think she needs a man trying to influence her when a man got her into this," Lori says. "I'm going with you to the meeting and I'm talking to her myself."

I reach for her hand and kiss it. "Yes, my queen."

She laughs. "If only that was how you replied to everything."

A few hours later, Lori and I are about to leave for Walker Security when Reid calls. I wave for Lori to shut my door and place him on speaker phone. "Lori and I are both here, Reid."

"Of course you are," he says. "You're like one person. I set the groundwork. The DA is 'thinking' about my offer and he wants to close. The sooner Lori goes there and convinces him that's what she wants, the better. As in now."

I glance at my watch. "It's two o'clock. We have a meeting at five. We can do it now."

"I need to talk to Ashley," Lori insists.

"I'll see if Royce can push back our meeting an hour," I say. "We'll try to work it out for this afternoon," I then tell Reid. "Otherwise it will be morning. I'll text you. Anything else I need to know?"

"No. Text me." He hangs up.

I dial Royce and get the FBI meeting moved back an hour and then he works some kind of five-minute magic to confirm the DA is in his own office. "I want you to go first," I tell Lori, right after texting Reid. "Take a taxi. I'll arrive right after you. We need to make this look like you snuck out to see the DA and I found out. Then, of course, I charge in to save you from him."

"That works," she says. "I'll head out now."

"Make sure I'm in the building before you go in to see him."

"Got it."

"If we're lucky, this is the beginning of the end of this for us. Then we let Royce and his team do their real magic and get rid of this DA before he hurts someone else."

"The beginning of the end is a new beginning," Lori says. "I like how that sounds." She heads for the door, and those words replay in mind: *The beginning of the end is a new beginning.*

That statement works only if the end is the end of our choosing. For us and Ashley, we need to ensure that's what happens. And we need to do it now, today.

Lori

I am remarkably calm as I step into the building where the District Attorney, Tom Milner, works. I text Cole before I work through the security process. By the time the security guard calls up to the DA's office to announce my presence, Cole has confirmed he's outside waiting for me to head upstairs before coming inside. I wait a full fifteen minutes before I'm cleared.

Nerves set in once I'm in the elevator, but I decide to use them in my favor. I want exactly what I'm going to say I want. I have no lie to tell this man. I tug on the jacket of my navy suit and smooth my skirt for no good reason. It's just a thing I do when I prepare for a confrontation, though this doesn't have to be that. The elevator dings and I exit to the lobby and the secretary is quick to greet me. "Mrs. Brooks, the District Attorney is waiting on you in his office." She motions to a door.

"Thank you." I quickly move forward and step inside a large office with heavy mahogany furnishings.

The man behind the desk is dark-haired, with a goatee and strong features, a spray of lines by his eyes. "Mrs. Brooks."

"Lori," I say. "And thank you for seeing me, Mr. District Attorney."

"Shut the door. Have a seat."

"Of course." I shut the door and claim one of two visitors' chairs in front of his desk.

"To what do I owe this pleasure?"

"I'm sure it's not a pleasure, but I do appreciate you indicating it as such. My husband is quite worried about me."

"As expected."

"He and my friends love me. I've had a bad few years. My father died. I dropped out of law school because my mother had a stroke. Life is good now and that means I have people who love me. That also makes them passionate about protecting me and attacking on my behalf. I need normal though. I just want to practice and fight the good fight. I'm asking them to back off."

He arches a brow. "Meaning what?"

"Meaning they were angry with you. I'm not. I mean, I can't dismiss the lawsuit. We're donating that money to the victims' families, but when that's done, I want it to just be done. No more fighting with you."

"What are you asking for?"

"Peace. I don't want us fighting with you over me. I want this over. I *need* it to be over. Please help this end. I can't settle for less than what is fair but let's just settle. We can hold a press conference and tell the world we're all going to fight the bad guys, not each other."

His line buzzes. "Mr. Brooks is here."

I sigh and press my hands to my face before looking at him. "I didn't want him here. I didn't tell him I was coming."

"Well, let's see if he's on the same page with you, because if he's not, what good is this conversation?" He punches the button on his phone. "Send Mr. Books in."

I stand up and in a few beats, Cole is in the door. "What the hell is this?" he demands.

I whirl around to face him and grab his arms. "I need us all to just end this, Cole. Please. If you love me, just let the lawsuit be it."

"He let Roger out without telling us."

"That was a clerical error," Tom replies.

"Bullshit," Cole growls and looks at me. "Leave us."

"Cole—"

"I need to speak to the DA alone."

"No," I say. "No, I won't leave. End this. End it for me."

"What do you want from me, Lori?"

"When we settle, we call a truce. We hold a press conference. We all support the victims of the murderer and their families. Then it's over. We live happily ever after and so does our District Attorney."

He stares at me long and hard with so much anger in his eyes that I know he wants to deny me this request, despite knowing that Royce is still going after him. Finally, though, he turns to the DA. "I'll agree if I'm happy with the settlement."

"You will praise me in the press conference," Tom says. "Do you understand?"

"I will not praise you," Cole says. "But I won't punch you now or ever." He takes my arm and leads me to the door.

A few minutes later we're on the street where we pause to talk, only to have Cole's cellphone ring. "Reid," he says answering the line, and in a matter of thirty seconds, he disconnects. "The DA agreed to four times his initial offer. He believes we've backed off. It's done. Or we're done. Now it's in Royce's hands." His cellphone rings again and he glances at the number. "Speaking of Royce." He answers the line and shock registers on his face. "When?" He pauses. "We'll be there in fifteen minutes." He disconnects. "The CIA just showed up at Royce's office and took Ashley."

LISA RENEE JONES

CHAPTER TWENTY-EIGHT

Cole

Lori and I enter the lobby of the Walker offices to be greeted by Royce Walker. "What the hell is going on, Royce?" I demand. "Where is Ashley? I'm her attorney. She has rights."

"Not under the Espionage Act, and that's what they stated when I said the same thing," he says, his hands settling on his hips. "I have a few good men who are ex-CIA. I have them working on answers."

"What will they do with her?" Lori asks. "Where will they take her?"

"If we're lucky, they'll question her and let her go."

Smith walks into the room and joins us. "Or they use her for bait for her ex," he adds grimly.

"Or that," Royce agrees.

"Did you get her to tell you anything?" Lori asks, focused on Smith.

"Just that she was a fool," he says. "Per her, not me. And that 'fool' comment seemed to cut deep. It could be about a broken heart, but my gut tells me there's more."

"I need a number to contact," I say. "Did they leave a card?"

"They flashed badges and I called them in before I let them take her. I can give you the main number, but it's not going to get you anywhere."

"I need that number," I say, and he reaches in this pocket and hands me the card, flipping it over, to show me the handwritten number on the back. "I knew you'd insist." He motions to the reception desk. "Use it or take my office. Whatever suits you."

"We won't be staying," I say, pulling my phone out of my pocket and walking toward the reception desk while Royce glances at Lori. "Coffee?"

"No, thanks," she says. "I'm a little too on edge. We just came from the DA's office and he already called Reid. The settlement is done, verbally at least. Once we have the signed paperwork, we're going to do a press conference with him."

Meanwhile, I have a machine I'm dealing with, and a million options that promise a human on the other line. I try the one I think will work and end up on hold.

"Is he convinced you've backed off?" Royce asks Lori of the DA.

"Yes," we both say at once, and she glances over her shoulder, giving me one of her perfect smiles. "And Cole was the perfect, angry husband who gave in for the love of his wife," she adds.

"I suspect that wasn't a hard job for him," Smith comments. "Even I know that and I haven't been around you two that much."

"Is there a way to get to a real human, Royce?" I ask.

"I got there because one of the agents punched in a code," he says. "I'll get answers for you through my men. They're unfortunately on high-risk jobs, and can't call until they have a safe moment, but we have other men with connections. We're working every angle. Go home. I'll call you when we know something."

"Make it soon," I say, guiding Lori toward the door.

"I can't believe this is really happening," Lori says. "They just *took* her."

"And I'm not sure we can save her."

"Save her from what?" she asks. "What is this?"

I open the door to the car we have waiting for us. "I don't know."

Lori slides into the car and I join her, giving the driver the office address before dialing Reese. "Where are you?"

"At the office. Why?

"I need you. We'll be there in fifteen minutes."

Two hours later, Lori, Cat, Reese and I are all in a conference room with phones in hand trying to get answers. We get nowhere. It's nearly ten when Royce calls and I put him on speaker. "Tell us something good."

"It's not good," Royce says. "One of my men talked to an insider. She's not even in the city any longer. He wouldn't say what her status is, be it witness or suspect."

"What if I hold a press conference?" I ask. "Will it pressure them to tell us where she's at?"

"If you do that," he says, "you tell the world her story that might be one she doesn't want told. There's more going on here than we know. Give us some time."

Cat quickly chimes in with, "The media is brutal. This might be over in twenty-four hours, but this may haunt her much longer if you take it public."

I share a look with Reese, who nods, before my gaze shifts to Lori, who nods, too. "Bluff, Royce. Tell them if I don't hear from her in twenty-four hours, we're going to the press. Tell them I only held off because you convinced me to."

"The CIA doesn't intimidate," Royce warns.

Lori speaks up, "But they might not know what we know. And they might not want everything they think we know public."

And there's the reason she was made for a courtroom. She knows how to find an angle.

"I'm on it," Royce says, hanging up.

"And now we wait," I say.

"No," Lori says. "Let's go to her apartment. She came back from Paris, where she was with this man, who was her fiancé. Maybe there's something there that tells us what's really going on."

Another good idea that has me standing up. "I'll have Royce's team get us in."

"We'll sit this one out," Reese says. "But I'm still waiting for that friend of mine that has a CIA contact. I'll let you know if he calls."

It turns out that Smith has a key to Ashley's place because of his part as her security detail. He meets us at her apartment and Lori and I wait impatiently while he unlocks the door. Lori squeezes my hand as he opens it as if she expects some kind of shock. Smith enters first and curses. "Holy fucking hell."

I enter behind him and curse right along with him as Lori whispers, "Oh my God."

The apartment is empty. As in completely empty.

Smith pulls his phone from his pocket and I hear, "Royce. Her apartment is wiped." He listens a few beats and then disconnects. "Either she's been put in witness protection or they really think she knows something or has something they need. They weren't taking any chances they'd miss it."

There is a dark spot forming in my chest, a heaviness on my shoulders. Ashley has no one in this world. I was supposed to protect her. Lori wraps her arms around me and looks up at me. "This isn't your fault."

I stare down at her, this woman who is my life, afraid that one day I will fail her as I have Ashley and I know this is a dangerous place for my mind to go. These demons are halfway back in their box. They need to go back in and stay in.

"It's the CIA, man," Smith says softly, and when my eyes meet his he says, "You didn't do this. You didn't cause this. And she's alive. I will make the promise to you now that I'll keep her that way. I'll find her."

There is something raw and emotional in his words, a sense of personal with Ashley that I've seen hints of before, that I am now certain runs deeper than a mere flirtation.

They've bonded. He cares. He's in her corner right along with us. "I'll hold you to that. Let us know if you hear anything. Right now, I need to take my wife home." I wrap my arm around Lori's shoulders and walk toward the door, wasting no time walking us into the hallway.

We are already walking toward the elevator when Lori asks, "Does he have your direct cellphone number?"

I stop walking. "Good question." I kiss her. "Let me run back and make sure." Eager to get my wife alone, and be home, I hurry back to the door, and open it to find Smith leaning on the window, his hands pressed to the glass, head low, torment rolling off of him. It hits me then that he must feel responsible. He was protecting her.

He shoves off the glass and turns to look at me. "They walked in and took her. You didn't do this." I tell him.

"I should have taken her underground. I felt it in my bones. I ignored it."

"She wouldn't have let you," I say.

"If I decided to take her underground, I wouldn't have given her an option any more than they did, only now it's them, not me."

I don't say more. I can't say more. I get it. I know what he feels. It's a small piece of what I have felt with Lori's attacks. "You have my number?"

"Yes. I have your number."

We stand there several beats, staring at each other and I turn and exit. Lori is waiting for me at the door, and I grab her, pull her to me and say, "I love you."

"I love you, too," she whispers, and then I don't care where we are. My mouth slants over hers, and I'm kissing her, hard and deep, possessiveness in every lick, stroke, and taste. I need to feel my wife. I need to know she's alive and well. And I need out of my head, to lose myself in every part of her. I tear my mouth from hers and lace my fingers with hers. "Let's go home."

CHAPTER TWENTY-NINE

Cole

Lori and I slide into the hired car waiting on us just outside of Ashley's building, and neither of us speak, not with the driver present. For me, the silence is both welcome and torture at the same time. There's an explosion brewing in me and only when Lori covers my hand on my leg do I realize how hard I'm squeezing it. I look at her and her green eyes cut through the shadows, understanding in their depths. She knows that I'm torturing myself right now. She knows that I'm blaming myself. No one in this world has ever known me well enough to know what I'm feeling. There was a period in my life, not so long ago, that I didn't want anyone to know me this well.

By the time we're in the thankfully empty elevator, the edge I'd felt in the car is growing sharper, while my thoughts are not. I pull Lori to me, her back to my front,

269

willing this feeling under control. I don't go dark often. I don't let myself ever have that little control, but the past two weeks have hit one of my hotspots, caring about people that can end up gone. Lori doesn't let me escape. She twists in my arms. "Cole—"

I cup her head and pull her mouth to mine. "Don't talk." I kiss her with a deep stroke of my tongue, and I feel her shock, her temporary surprise before she moans and melts into me, but she knows. She sees what I'm doing. I don't want to talk. I want to fix things. I want Ashley back. I want to keep her safe. I want to get this edge off and that means I need my wife, now.

The elevator dings and I take her hand, leading her from the car, toward our apartment. I don't look at her. I don't want those pretty, all-knowing eyes to compel me to talk. I open the door and lead us inside and the minute I pull Lori into our apartment, my mouth is on hers again, and it's not a gentle kiss. It's a deep, intense, passion that is all about taking, burying, *fucking*. I want and need one thing right now and it all comes back to her. The taste of her, the sound of her pleasure, the heat of her body next to mine.

I let her know. With my mouth, my hands. The rough, impatient way I tug at her clothes, and peel away my jacket, but outside of unzipping my pants, I'm focused on her. I want her naked and that's where this goes. Her in her high heels, thigh highs and nothing else. Me turning her to the door, pressing her against it and smacking her backside. My fingers caressing her sex, tweaking her nipple, sinking inside her, and then finally, I turn her to face me again. I'm not even sure which one of us pulls my cock from my pants, but it's not soon enough. I drag her leg to my hip and I press into the slick heat of her body that is absolute-fucking-heaven. I don't even think about waiting. I don't want to go slow or be gentle. I drive into her, thrusting hard and fast. She gasps and closes her fingers around my shirt sleeves, while I lean in and kiss her, a deep, possessive taking that has me lifting her.

Her knees are at my hips, my hand cupping her backside, while the other splays between her shoulder blades. She is gripping my shirt again and I shackle her hips, urging her to lean back, to take more, to know that I will hold her, that I won't let her fall, to trust me. She does it without hesitation, arching her back even as she leans away from me while pressing into me. We are frenzied, wild, fierce, and when she stiffens, that look of ultimate anticipation on her face, I drag her to me and hold her close. She shatters around me, milking my cock with hard spasms, and I go along for the tumble into release right along with her. She trembles and I quake, and somehow we end up on the ground, me against the wall, and her in my lap, collapsed on top of me.

I hold her and seconds, maybe minutes, tick by before she whispers, "We've never had front door sex. That worked for me. How about you?"

I laugh. "Yes, sweetheart. It worked for me."

She presses on my chest and leans back to look at me. "Did it?"

"Yes," I assure her, realizing now how much less on edge I am. "No one else could take me from where I was to laughing about front door sex but you."

"You know this isn't your fault, right?"

"I'm still inside you. Is this really the best time to have this conversation?"

"I'm pretty sure it's the only way to have this conversation based on how you were in the car."

My lips curve. "Well, every conversation is better when I'm inside you, but if we stay like this long enough we won't be talking."

"You aren't that fast," she teases. "Pretty fast sometimes, but—" She sobers. "Cole—"

I pull her to me and kiss her. "I know it's not my fault, but Ashley has no one in this world. Somehow, when I wanted to have no one in this world, I have you, and with you I seem to have realized I have a richer life in the way of people I care for than I realized." I kiss her temple and stand up with both of us, my hamstrings burning with the effort to the point I moan.

"You should put me down." Lori laughs when I start walking.

"I don't want to put you down," I say and it's true. Holding her and staying inside her the rest of the night sounds pretty damn good.

Inevitably though, I do set her down once we're in the bathroom at the sink where I hand her a towel and grab her robe from behind the door. "How about a pizza?"

"Okay," she says, slipping on her robe.

I kiss her and help her to the floor. I grab my phone and place our order with a late-night joint we know well. In the process I walk to the bedroom and ultimately the window, overlooking the starless dark city. I've just stuck my phone back in my pocket when Lori appears by my side, stepping between me and the glass, where she leans on the clear surface. "I get it," she says. "A life rich in people means you can lose those people. You know how I feel about this. Death is that thing you can't control. I can't control it. It's terrifying. It's why I panic when my phone rings, for fear it's about my mother again."

"I can't believe I've never asked you about that story," I say, my hand settling on her waist. "How did you find out about your father and your mother?"

"With my father, I was in the law school library when a security guard came and got me, of all people. I knew when he stopped by my side that it was bad. I knew. They took me into an office and a nurse had to tell me because my mother was incapable of speaking." She cuts her gaze and I can almost feel her lose her breath before she looks at me. "I had to be strong. She was—she was bad."

"When did you cry?"

"I don't remember when I cried, Cole. I know I did, but it wasn't at the funeral. I found this cold spot to live inside."

"What about your mother's stroke?"

She inhales and lets it out. "In the middle of a mock trial. The teacher pulled me aside. The trip to get from school to the city was hell."

My forehead settles on hers. "You're never going to be alone again. I promise."

She leans back to look at me. "You can't promise that. I can't promise that to you either, so let's just promise that we are going to crazy love each other every single second."

"Yes," I say, my voice low, rough. "Every second."

Her fingers curl on my jaw. "Ashley is alone. You're right. We have to help her. But how?"

"How," I repeat when a thought hits me.

"Houston."

"What about Houston?"

"I don't know. It just feels like an answer. It's where she's from. It's where she met her fiancé." I pull my phone from my pocket and dial Royce, placing him on speaker.

"Nothing new," he says.

"I assume you'd looked for details on the fiancé in Houston?"

"Yes. His apartment is empty. It's a dead end."

"Her friends in Houston might know something," I suggest.

"What friends?" Royce asks.

"Hell if I know, but I'm in between cases. I need to go down there anyway. I'll see what I can find out." I arch a brow at Lori and she nods. "We'll go to Houston in the morning."

"I have a man in Houston. He can meet you." We disconnect.

"We have a plan," Lori says. "We go to Houston. A plan feels good."

"Houston it is," I say, and for the first time, Lori and I will face one of the reasons I left Houston: My dead father and my past, but I welcome this. Tonight, we've proven we still have much to learn about each other and embracing every second together means holding nothing back.

CHAPTER THIRTY

Lori

We wake to no news about Ashley at all.

By ten in the morning, I'm already dressed in a blue suit dress and Cole is in a perfectly fitted blue pinstriped suit, looking good enough to eat. Unfortunately, there is no time for me to show him how much I approve. By eight, we're seated on a private jet to Houston. Once we're settled into our seats, I let the magnitude of the words "private plane" hit me. "Are the skills of these pilots regulated?" I ask.

Cole laughs and laces his fingers with mine. "Our pilot is an ex-special ops guy. I've flown with him. We really do need to consider flying lessons for you."

"No," I say. "I'm fine."

His cellphone rings, while a flight attendant offers us coffee that I eagerly accept, as does Cole. "Alex," he says. "Yes. We're coming to you for unexpected reasons. I still want you to meet Reese and see the offices, but if you can do dinner tonight I can make sure it's worth everyone's time for you to come to New York." He listens a minute. "Yes. We'll leave Friday morning so you can hitch a ride if you want to. I have a private plane." I doctor my coffee my way, as he adds, "Yes. Perfect. We'll see you there." He disconnects. "Dinner tonight at a spot by the courthouse. He's in court this afternoon."

"How do you know Alex?" I ask, sipping my coffee as he does the same.

"We met at a judge's retirement party, and we both had a challenge with a particular ADA. We ended up exchanging notes and we became friends. Not close friends, but friends. He's a good guy, and a killer in the courtroom."

"How old is he?"

"Thirty-six."

"How long has he been practicing and where?" I ask.

"Since he graduated, and he went with a big firm but left to work on his own two years ago. That's not always easy going. It takes money to operate, and it can pressure you into taking cases you don't want to take."

"And that's been an issue for him?"

"Yes," he says, "and why so many questions?"

"You and Reese are perfect together. I just don't want a third wheel to mess with the mojo."

He laughs and kisses me. "You and Cat protect our mojos, but thank you, sweetheart. We need Alex and he'll be in Houston anyway."

"But partners make decisions."

"He won't be a controlling partner. At least not initially." He sobers. "I don't want to be in Houston and I might have suggested you be a backup for that office, but I don't want you in Houston, either. Not if it can be avoided."

There is something dark and turbulent in his stare. I reach out and touch his cheek. "I'm thankful to get to see this part of your life, Cole."

"The past. You're seeing the past, Lori."

"I know, but it's still a part of you."

"It's the past," he says again. "You, now, you're the future." The engine revs to life and before I can ask anything else, Cole kisses me, and the plane is moving. In a matter of minutes, we've lifted off, on our way to Houston. On our way to Cole's life before me.

Cole

Once we arrive in Houston, we settle into a hired car. "Once we get to the office," I say, "I'm going to have to deal with the asshole running the place into the ground."

"I'll introduce myself around and see who knows what about Ashley," Lori offers.

"I hate that I don't know more about who she was friends with."

"Trials are consuming, Cole," she reminds me. "You knew about the man in her life. It was a whirlwind romance. I doubt anyone knows him. From what we know, he wasn't someone that let that happen unless he wanted it to happen."

Lori

He doesn't respond and I understand. If I were in his place, I'd blame myself, too. Cole and I are alike in this; we need to protect those around us. I love that he wants to protect me, but I will never let him hold the world up alone, just as the recent days have taught me that Cole will never allow me to hold it up on my own either.

A few minutes later, we step inside the Houston high-rise that houses the offices and when we exit to the lobby, I stop as I stare at the name Summer and Brooks etched into the wall, with a list of partners beneath it. "Did it used to say Brooks and Brooks?"

"No," Cole says, his hand settling between my shoulders. "My father would never have shared that honor with me or anyone. And I didn't want my name on the wall while he was in charge." He turns to face me, his hands on my shoulders. "I'm not him," he says solemnly.

"I know that."

"You will hear stories."

"About you or him?"

"Him."

"Then why do I sense there is more?"

"It's hard to hear what a monster he was, and not wonder if it's in the blood."

"I don't plan on gambling away all of our money like my father. I'm quite confident you don't plan on becoming an arrogant ass."

"Now I'm not arrogant? Because you said I was."

"Okay," I concede, "you are, in fact, arrogant, but lovably so and if you act like an ass, I'll kick you in yours."

He leans in and whispers. "As long as I get to spank yours."

As many intimate, erotic things as I've done with this man, I still have these shy, wonderful moments with him that curl my toes and heat my cheeks. "I love when you blush," he adds, with a low laugh, lacing his fingers with mine. "Come. Let's go rule this part of our world together."

It's not long before I've met the front office and administrative staff and a few attorneys Cole seems to be fond of before he ends up behind closed doors with the man who we have long known wants to organize a hostile takeover. I don't actually meet the man. I'm distracted by conversation elsewhere when it happens.

Being on my own is not uncomfortable. Everyone is friendly and while Cole believes I will hear horrible stories about his father, I hear praise for Cole. He's nothing like his father is a common statement. Help is another. Most people are aware that there has been a decline in the office in Cole's absence. A few people ask about Ashley and how she's doing with us in New York, but no one really knows her. She was a loner, at least at the office.

On the pretense of Ashley asking me to find a missing item for her, I search her desk and still find nothing. She cleaned it out well before she left, or someone cleaned it out like they did her apartment. Cole is in his meeting for so long that I hole up in his old office that is empty but for the furnishings now. It's after five and I've settled onto the couch with my MacBook when Royce calls me. "Do you have news on Ashley?" I ask eagerly.

"Where is Cole? He's not answering his line." Cole walks into the room, owning it the minute he arrives, power radiating off him that I've come to understand. He's not quite come down from a battle, but he won the fight. "Royce," I say to him and he shuts the door, walking my direction.

"Put him on speaker," he says, joining me on the couch.

"I'm here," Cole says. "I know you've been calling. I've been in a meeting. Where do we meet up with your man?"

"I've been told to step back from this," Royce announces.

I frown and my eyes meet Cole's as he asks, "By who?"

"The CIA and the FBI," Royce says. "We won't stop pushing, but we need to be discreet and back off. You guys need to back off before you end up pulled into this in a way that won't allow you an exit."

A chill runs down my spine. "Okay, but what does that mean for Ashley?"

"She's safe," Royce assures us. "Maybe she won't be if we bring attention to her."

"Did they say that?" Cole asks, his tone sharp.

"Yes. They say they're protecting her."

"What does that mean?" I ask.

"Protection," Royce says, "can mean many things. Come see me when you get back."

"Tomorrow," Cole says. "We still need to go by her apartment. A neighbor might know something about that man she was with."

"Let my men handle that," Royce says. "We will handle it and Cole, I wouldn't want my woman anywhere near this."

Cole sucks in air. "I'll call you when we land tomorrow." He disconnects. "We aren't done. We won't give up."

"Agreed," I say, making sure he knows I'm standing by him, holding up the world right now.

He studies me a moment. "How was your afternoon?"

"No one spoke of your father. I got the impression the living asshole in charge of the office affected them to present day and stirred the past. They want help."

"That's why we need to recruit Alex." But he's not thinking about Alex. He's watching me.

I lean forward and brush his jaw. "They said what I know and one day you will, too. You're not him."

He is stone in response, but even in the hardness of his stare, I can see the demons of his past. The pain that lives there and in this place for him. Abruptly, he pulls me to him and kisses me. "We can't be home soon enough. Let's get the hell out of here."

Home.

Our home.

The place we don't have to hold up anything but each other.

He stands to offer me his hand when his cellphone rings again. He glances down at the screen and frown. "No caller ID." He answers. "Cole Brooks." His eyes jolt. "Ashley?"

I jump to my feet. "Is she okay? Where is she?"

He puts her on speaker. "I have Lori here, too. Where are you?"

"I love you both," she says, her voice strong, "but you need to back off. I'm okay. I'm leaving. I have to go."

"Witness protection?" I ask, sharing Cole's concerned look.

"Yes. And I'm not supposed to say that. You will force me to hide even deeper. I can't contact you. Cole, you're like a brother. Lori, you were fast becoming a sister. But I'm gone now. Forget me or you'll get me killed." She disconnects.

CHAPTER THIRTY-ONE

Lori

Once Cole and I exit the Houston office, I stop him right before we enter the car waiting on us, concerned about privacy. "Should we call Royce about Ashley's call?"

"Royce already told us what she told us," he says. "In fact, I'm quite certain he was giving us a heads up about that call, but yes." He eyes his watch. "I'll text him in a discreet way from the car."

I nod and he opens the door for me. Once we're settled inside, he directs our driver and then sends the text. Royce replies instantly, and Cole shows me the message that reads: *She's safe. That's what matters.*

"She really is in that program," I say, choosing my words carefully.

"Yes. I believe she is."

"Can she ever get out?"

"Doubtful," he says, kissing my hand. "I think we said our final goodbyes upstairs."

"Me too," I say, feeling sad and relieved at the same time. "She's safe," I repeat. "That is ultimately what matters."

"Except that someone stripped away her life."

"Maybe she'll find a new, happy one," I suggest. "Like we did."

"Like we did," he repeats, his eyes warm on mine.

I settle my head on his shoulder, silently imagining a fairy tale for Ashley with her own Prince Charming, praying it comes true. We arrive at the restaurant only a few minutes later, and Cat sends me a text as we exit the car. "Cat's holding a surprise birthday party for Reese at the house Saturday night. It's a last-minute idea she had, she says. She wants us to come and Alex is invited."

Cole's hand settles on my back. "Let's go convince him he needs to be at that party."

We step inside the cozy entrance with stone beneath our feet, and wine bottles lining the walls left and right. "The pizza is the best," he says, as we wait our turn for the hostess.

"Pizza it is, then," I say, and my stomach is growling when it's finally our turn to be seated. Cole and I step forward, and the hostess leaves us at the podium to check on our table. We maneuver to the side of the line when a man steps between us and Cole and I are momentarily separated.

Cole offers me his hand to pull me close, but suddenly a beautiful brunette throws her arms around him, and my hand falls from his reach. "My God, Cole. I thought you left." She leans back, her deep cleavage right smack in the middle of the two of them, her smile sexy. "Let's catch up, preferably not here."

Cole untangles himself from her arms. "Shelly," he says, looking for me, and literally taking a sideways step to catch my finger. "This is Lori, my wife. Lori this is Shelly Waller. She's a corporate attorney that I've known for some years."

Her eyes go wide. "Wife? Oh God." She holds up her hands. "I'm sorry." She looks at me. "Lori, I'm sorry. I would never—I wouldn't—this is very awkward."

"It's okay," I say, and then I smile. "Well, not really, but I'll live."

She laughs nervously. "Right. Okay." She looks a Cole. "I'll leave now." She eyes Cole. "Congrats." She disappears.

"Mr. Brooks," the hostess says. "Your table is ready."

Cole looks at me. "I'll explain." His arm wraps my shoulders and he kisses me before we follow the waitress, and I try to decide what I feel. This woman was clearly intimate with Cole, and it wasn't a one-time thing. But he was free then. He was a gorgeous, successful man who, of course, had women lining up for him. I have no reason to be bothered by this. He's my husband.

We settle into a half-moon-shaped booth, and once we're alone, Cole's hand comes down on my leg and he drags me close. "She was just someone I knew."

"She's very pretty."

"She *is* very pretty, and yet I had no desire to see her or anyone else from the moment I met you. And that, *my wife*, pissed me off."

I blanch. "Pissed you off? Why did it piss you off?"

"Because you left me and I had no idea how to find you."

"Oh," I laugh. "That."

"Yes. That."

"How well did you know Ms. Very Pretty?"

"Does it matter?"

"Yes," I say. "It does."

"I had a couple of women I dated casually."

"You mean a couple of women you fucked?"

His grip tightens on my leg. "Now I only fuck you, as often as I can."

"I'm glad we don't live here."

"Me too, sweetheart," he says softly, his mood darkening. "Me too. And for the record, you're beautiful and the only reason I agreed that she's pretty is I wanted you to understand that it didn't matter. You mattered then and you damn sure matter now."

The waiter appears at that very moment and Cole leans in and kisses me, and the rush of heat flooding my body isn't about the kiss, well, not the kiss alone. It's about this man and all the things he makes me feel and want and need. And now I know I can have all of those things that I still feel, want, and need just as much. Cole orders a bottle of wine after we discuss our options, and no sooner does the man disappear then the hostess appears, leaving us a tall, dark and good looking man in a gray suit with a neatly trimmed goatee.

"What's a guy got to do to get a whiskey sour around here?" he asks, claiming the seat on the other side of the booth from us.

"Hey, man," Cole says. "Good to see you."

They do some guy shake that isn't a shake at all and then Alex is fixing me in a rich brown stare. "And you must be Lori."

"I'm definitely not Shelly," I say before I can stop myself.

Both men laugh and Alex says, "No. You are not. I know Shelly, and Cole was never going to marry that woman."

The waiter appears with our wine, and a few minutes later, all three of us have drinks in front of us and Alex cuts to the chase. "I know why you want me. You have an asshole running the Houston location."

"While that's true, that's not why," Cole says. "We want to rule the world. I believe you can help us do that."

I sit back and listen to them talk, enjoying watching my husband negotiate as much as I enjoy watching him in the courtroom. He needs to be back in a courtroom. "What's the offer?" Alex finally asks.

"You can buy in as third in line."

"Why not equal?"

"I put in fifty million. If you want to meet that, you're equal," Cole says.

Alex arches a brow. "I'll go a few million tops and we both know you didn't buy in for fifty million."

"No," Cole concedes, "but I set-up a fund for the company, readily available in that sum. Money you'd have available. Are you in?"

"I want to meet Reese," he says. "I'll hitch that ride with you, but I have a trial starting next week. It's big and I'm all the way in on it until it's over."

"We'll make it work," Cole says.

"What's the case?" I ask.

"Real estate investor accused of killing his wife to get out the sizable divorce settlement and then burying her under a rental house," he says. "Her sister did it. I'm going to prove it."

I start asking questions, intrigued by the case, and before long our glasses are empty and stomachs full. Alex looks at me and then Cole. "If you had to go the damn marriage route, at least you picked one with a brain."

"You don't like marriage?" I ask.

"Not the marrying kind," he says dryly. "Not the family kind. I work too hard and too long, with no time for distractions, like women who need and want more than what I need and want."

"Which is what?" I ask.

"A moment that passes without a mention of white picket fences so I can get back to work."

"And you're thirty-six?" I ask.

"Look out," Cole says. "She's going to tell you that—"

"That there must be something wrong with me," Alex supplies. "There is and I like it that way." He glances at his watch. "What time are we leaving in the morning?"

"Nine," Cole says, giving him details.

Alex winks at me. "Don't be trying to fix me up or the deal is off." He motions to Cole. "He likes me just how I am." He leaves and I turn to Cole.

"What's his real story?"

"Foster child shoved from bad home to bad home, but he's brilliant, as in *really* brilliant. He got into Harvard with a full scholarship. Landed a big firm job. Made some cash, invested well, and then started his firm."

"So he's broken."

"Aren't we all?"

"Yes," I agree. "But he's alone and broken."

"And so was I until I found you. Let's go to the hotel." He tosses cash on the table and helps me to my feet.

About fifteen minutes later, we pull up in front of Ashley's old building. We don't go in. We just sit there a few minutes, talking about her, and laughing at her big personality. We say our goodbyes. When we finally head back to the hotel, we enter our room, and stand at the window, me in front of Cole, his arms wrapped around me. We don't make love and it doesn't feel wrong.

We just enjoy the fact that we're together.

We are no longer alone.

It feels like we are settling into a new place together, one that isn't just about passion and intensity, though we are those things. But here, now, we've created a shelter, a small space in the universe that is only ours, where it's safe and calm. One we've relaxed inside, as we've escaped fear and doubt and even pain. We've found more than love. We've found peace, the kind that doesn't care what hell rages around us. We can step into this space together, and everything else fades. There is just us.

I'm pretty sure that means we've finally fit all the broken pieces of our lives into one perfect heart that we now share.

CHAPTER THIRTY-TWO

Lori

Cole and I dress in work attire for the trip home to New York City to allow us to go straight to the office when we land, him in a blue suit and me in a simple, travel-easy black dress. We're settled into the leather seats of a private plane, both doctoring our coffee when I have this surreal moment of this being my life. I'm living my dream, sitting next to the man I love who is my husband, on my way to New York City, where we will go to work, and I love my job. I'm doing what I wanted to do. I'm doing what I always wanted to do and I'm doing it with this man.

I reach up and stroke his cleanly shaven jaw and he catches my hand, kissing it, giving me an inquiring look. "What are you thinking?"

"That daring to have a one night stand was a really good decision."

His eyes warm and soften. "Yes. It was."

He kisses me, his hand coming down on my face in that possessive, wonderful way of his, his tongue licking into my mouth, only to have his cellphone ring. Cole groans this deep, masculine tormented groan that is sexy as hell, partially because it's his distress at the interruption. "It could be Alex. I better take it." He grabs his phone and glances at the screen. "Reid."

"Oh, good," I say. "Hopefully he finally finished negotiating with the DA."

He answers the call and I listen in with little success, but thankfully I don't have to wait long. The call is fast and Cole's relaxed demeanor tells me the news is good even before he says, "It's done. Reid's emailing me a final look at the contract, it won't be long before we sign and release the settlement proceeds to the victims' families."

"What about a press conference?" I ask.

"Reid will set it up quickly once we ink, that way we get the press attention off of us right after we make the deal," he says. "I'd rather let them burn themselves out next week during working hours."

"I'll forgot about the press *after* the press conference," I say. "I'm sure we'll have a good week of hell, but it will be worth it. You did a good thing for the victims' families, Cole."

"*We* did a good thing," he amends. "Now we hold Royce to his word and make sure he takes down the DA which," he adds, "we're going to need to share with Alex before this plane takes off. I should have addressed it at dinner and I didn't. He needs to know the path we're traveling."

It's right about then that Alex walks onto the plane, and a few minutes later, we're sitting at a lounge table in the back of the plane with the DA bombshell hanging in the air. Alex smiles. "If you didn't have balls of steel," he says, "I wouldn't be on this plane."

From there, the rest of the ride only gets better. Alex and Cole get along well and soon the three of us are talking about their old cases, Alex's current case, and the future of the firm. Alex is friendly with a good sense of humor, but I get the sense that I see this because he trusts me by way of Cole. I don't believe many see this side of him. He's hard beneath this friendly encounter with an edge that feels gritty in a street boxer kind of way. He's a fighter in every way, hard to the core, ready for war. That has me wondering if that's not exactly why I have no doubt he is an opponent to be reckoned with.

Once we land in New York City, we head straight to the office where Cole, Alex, and Reese hang out behind closed doors. I, in turn, sit down at Ashley's desk and look for clues I know I shouldn't look for. She's gone now. She's safe. I have to accept that. I find only one thing that feels significant. A piece of paper where she's scribbled over and over: *Why? Why? Why?* I pray she has those answers now, that she at least has that peace of mind, even if the answers aren't good answers. Maybe the man she loved *really did* love her.

With the party Saturday night, and Alex here now, I call my mother and arrange breakfast for Saturday morning at her new place. I then call a temp service and line up interviews to replace Ashley for Monday. I deliver this news to Maria, who arches a brow. "What happened to Ashley?"

"The relocation wasn't the right one for her," I say cautiously. "Which I hate, but we'll suffer through it."

She doesn't look convinced, but I don't give her a chance to ask more questions. I grab all of Cole's messages and head back to his office, where I weed through the ones I can handle, and pull out the ones I know he needs to deal with today. Next, I sit down at his conference table and go through the caseload his team is handling and look for the red flags he needs to address. Most of the staff is gone when Cole walks into the office. "Alex and Reese just left for dinner alone. They need to make sure they connect one-on-one."

DIRTY RICH CINDERELLA STORY: EVER AFTER

"How do you feel about it?" I ask as he sits down next to me.

"Like it's magic. This is what we need. He'll take Houston to the places I would have had I stayed, which means taking on the state of Texas and beyond."

His office phone buzzes. "Cole."

"Yes, Julia?" he says to the receptionist.

"There's a woman here asking for Lori, but ah—I think you both need to come here—" She lowers her voice. "Now. *Come now.*"

Both of our eyes go wide and we're on our feet in two flat seconds. We cross the office side by side. "Do you think it's a reporter over the Roger thing? Or maybe a reporter that found out I met with the DA?"

"A reporter wouldn't surprise me," he agrees.

We reach the lobby and find Julia standing, waiting on us. "She's in the conference room. She says she needs immediate representation and she's got blood down her neck. I don't think she knows. Do you want me to call the police?"

I look at Cole, a question in my eyes. "We'll call the police," he says. "Just not yet." He looks at Julia. "We'll handle it." He eyes me. "Let's go talk to her. We'll call the police with her, regardless of whether we represent her or not."

I nod and we round the reception desk and walk down a hallway to enter the conference room. The woman is facing the window but turns at our entry. She's pretty, brunette, petite, mid-thirties—maybe forty—but her hair is a bit wild and her pink blouse is missing a button. Cole shuts the door. "I want to hire you, Lori," she says, glancing at Cole and then me. "I need a woman. Only a woman can understand. I need client-attorney privilege."

"We need to know the facts of the case," Cole says, "and we need to know before we commit to represent you."

She cuts her gaze and when she looks at us again, tears welling in her eyes. "I'm Jenna Reynolds. My husband is Mike Reynolds, as in the famous sportscaster. I killed him. He was hitting me again—again, he just—he hit me all the time and I didn't mean to do it." Her voice lifts on the final words. She sucks in air and exhales. "I grabbed for something to get him off me and I hit him. I don't even know what it was. I just reached. His head—his head started—bleeding." She yanks up her blouse and there's massive bruising down her ribs, some yellow and some dark black, like she's taken multiple beatings at random times. "There are plenty more. My back. My head, but you can't see that. He hit me in places that no one would see." She grabs the back of a chair. "I didn't call the police. I saw Lori on TV. I saw her closing arguments. I need help. He's

DIRTY RICH CINDERELLA STORY: EVER AFTER

powerful. He's friends with the police commissioner. Please help."

I step forward and press my hands to the chair across from her. "Why didn't you leave him?"

"He threatened to ruin my mother, to bankrupt her, and I believed he would. She—she has investments and—he could have done worse, I believed that, too. She's all I have."

My gut knots. Like my mother was for me before Cole. Cole's hand comes down on my arm. "Let's go talk."

I nod. "We'll be right back."

I turn and exit the room with Cole on my heels. The minute we're in the hallway and the conference room door shuts, I face Cole. "I want this case. I know the police commissioner might be a problem, but Cole—"

"It's your case, Lori," he says. "It's the one. It's *your* case."

"She needs you. I'm still too green. I know this. I'm objective."

"Anyone who has you or me has us both, but she wants you. This is your case to lead."

"You want me to *lead*?"

"Yes. I do, and she does, too."

"Am I ready?"

He kisses my hand. "You were born ready, sweetheart."

"I need you on this," I say.

"I'll second."

"You can't second. You own the firm."

"I will happily second to you and not because you're my wife, but because she does need a woman. As another female, you'll give her credibility. If you believe in her, the jury can, too."

"I want to take it, but can we handle the police?"

"Damn straight we can handle the police."

He pulls me to him. "This is your dream, Lori. This is your time to shine. Let's go back inside and rescue this woman. The way you rescued your mother."

"The way you rescued me."

"You just let me come along for the ride. You rescued you. I just fell in love."

"You did so much more," I say, "and I'll detail that for you tonight, when we're alone. You saved me." I kiss him, this man who is always lifting me up, never pushing me down, or holding me back.

"As you did me, Lori. Let's go save someone else."

And together we enter the conference room again to do just that: save someone else, to save a life the way we saved each other.

CHAPTER THIRTY-THREE

Lori

Saturday morning, Cole and I arrive at my mother's new apartment which is off the Hudson River, both of us dressed in jeans and the new Summer and Brooks T-shirts that we just had made; mine pink, and his navy. "I have no idea why I'm nervous," I say, as we ride up in the elevator. "I've met Joe. I've even been to the apartment, so I've seen it. It's stunning."

Cole pulls me close. "Not since the day she moved in. You love your mother. Your biggest fear has been her getting hurt again."

"Yes. I love her. I'm so afraid he'll hurt her."

"Today's good then," he says. "You need to find peace with her new life."

The elevator dings and I pant out a breath. "And here we go."

"It'll be good."

I nod and we exit into the hallway. Once we're at the door, I ring the bell and my mother answers almost immediately, and she's radiant. Her brown hair is long and shiny, her green eyes alight with happiness. Her petite frame fit. "Honey!" she hugs me and then moves to Cole. "My other honey now."

Cole laughs and embraces her before she waves us in. "Joe is in the kitchen slaving away. Come." She heads down the long hallway, white tile beneath our feet and we enter the living area that is an open concept with the kitchen, a wall of windows allowing the water to become the centerpiece of the room.

"Hey, everyone!" Joe calls out, scooping pancakes onto a plate from a skillet on the stove smack in the center of a large, black granite island.

My mother joins him and she's tiny compared to Joe, who is a good six-foot-three and fit, with muscles that go on forever, while his goatee is flecked with gray to match his hair.

Cole and I join them, and Joe really is a great guy. He and Cole start talking and the rapport between the men is instant. A few minutes later, we sit down to eat. "So, Joe," I say. "You're an architect. That's very interesting. How did you get interested in design work?"

"I was young and in the special forces and happened to rescue a rather famous architect. We were in hiding together for months. He stirred my interest, taught me skills that he said should have taken much longer to learn and I was hooked. When I got out, I went to school and the rest is history. I designed this building."

"He's incredible," my mother says, stars in her eyes. Too many stars. They're still new.

"Have you been married before?" I ask.

"Yes," he says. "Happily. She died. And I was alone a long time until I met your mother. Which is why I don't intend to lose her. I've asked her to marry me."

I suck in air and Cole's hand squeezes my leg. "What?"

"I love her very much."

My mother reaches into her pocket and pulls out her ring, holding it up, and then sticking it on her finger. "I didn't want you to see it until we told you." She holds it out and it's a stunning solitaire. And big. Really big. "I love it. Do you love it?"

I look at Joe, his eyes holding mine, and I let myself see what is there. Let myself see the love. I let myself let go of the past. I turn my attention to my mother. "It's gorgeous. I do love it. And I'm so happy for you." I hug her and hug her and hug her.

"I want to get married in the Hamptons," she says. "We love it. We'd like to use your place there, now that we know it's yours. Can we?"

"We'd be honored to host your wedding," Cole says.

"Yes," I agree. "Honored. When?"

"The sooner the better," Joe says. "But I want it to be special for your mother."

She looks at him. "For us."

"For us, baby," he says, and the endearment both punches me in the chest and makes me smile. He's not my father, but I believe Joe is happiness for my mother. I believe he's her Prince Charming. Like Cole is mine.

A long time later, when we are at home, I tell him just that. "You are my Prince Charming."

He laughs. "Do I get to be in charge then? I mean, if I'm a prince and all."

"Don't get any ideas."

"I do have some ideas," he says lifting me and carrying me up the stairs, and setting me on the chair in our bedroom, in front of the window before going down on a knee. "Let me show you some of my ideas." He pulls a black box from under the chair and sets it in my lap. "Open it and pick your pleasure."

Curious I open the box and find all kinds of sexy items I've never dared or even considered using. "Scared?" he asks.

"No," I say. "This is you. I will do anything or go anywhere with you."

"Is that right?"

"Yes." I set the box aside and lace my fingers at his neck. "You're only a Prince Charming because I trust you that much. And trust is everything."

"You," he says, stealing a kiss, "are everything." He pulls me to him and we go down on the rug, the box forgotten. There's just us, and no matter what we face, no matter who we battle, the District Attorney included, we can't lose, because we have each other. *We are everything*, and for the first time in my life, letting someone else be part of my everything is safe. It's perfect. I really do have my happily ever after.

The end

———— ❧❦ ————

There's more Dirty Rich—Reid's book: Dirty Rich Obsession is available now, as well as my newest release:

Dirty Rich Betrayal! Keep reading for an excerpt from both books, plus DON'T MISS MY UPCOMING BRAND-NEW FILTHY DUET!

Book one, THE BASTARD, is available for pre-order and will be out on November 14th!

LEARN MORE HERE:

https://filthyduet.weebly.com/

I'm the bastard child, son to the mistress, my father's backup heir to the Mitchell empire. He sent me to Harvard. I left and became a Navy SEAL, but I'm back now, and I finished school on my own dime. I'm now the right hand man to Grayson Bennett, the billionaire who runs the Bennett Empire. I'm now a few months from being a billionaire myself. I don't need my father's company or his love. My "brother" can have it. I will never go back there. I will never be the mistake my father made, the way he was the mistake my mother made.

And then she walks in the door, the princess I'd once wanted more than I'd wanted my father's love. She wants me to come back. She says my father needs to be saved. I don't want to save my father but I do want her. Deeply. Passionately. More than I want anything else.

But she's The Princess and I'm The Bastard. We don't fit. We don't belong together and yet she says he needs me, that she needs me. We're like sugar and spice, we don't mix, but I really crave a taste. Just one. What harm can just one taste do?

There are a TON of Dirty Rich books forthcoming this year, and into 2019! Be sure you're up to date on all things Dirty Rich by visiting:

https://dirtyrich.lisareneejones.com

SERIES READING ORDER

Dirty Rich One Night Stand (Cat & Reese book 1)
Dirty Rich Cinderella Story (Lori & Cole book 1)
Dirty Rich Obsession (Reid & Carrie book 1)
Dirty Rich Betrayal (Mia and Grayson book 1)
Dirty Rich Cinderella Story: Ever After (Lori & Cole book 2)
Dirty Rich One Night Stand: Two Years Later (Cat & Reese book 2)
Dirty Rich Obsession: All Mine (Reid & Carrie book 2)
Dirty Rich Neighbor (Gabe's story)

EXCERPT FROM DIRTY RICH OBSESSION

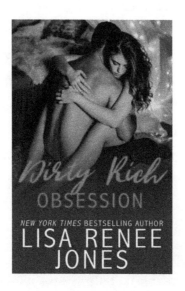

Reid

I want this woman.

I want her in a bad way, and my tongue licks hungrily into her mouth even as I tighten my grip on her hair. Her hand is warm on my chest, but her elbow is stiff, her entire body is stiff, and I don't accept this from her. I want her submission. I want her to admit she wants like I want, so I deepen the kiss, my hand settling between her shoulder blades, molding her close.

She moans into my mouth, a sexy, aroused sound, but she still fights me. She still shoves weakly at my chest, and her eyes meet mine. "This is just—"

"Hate sex," I supply. "Works for me." My mouth slants over hers again, and this time, she doesn't hold back. She kisses me like she did in that hotel room, her hands sliding under my jacket, over my shirt, and I am hot and hard and ready to be inside her.

I reach up and skim her jacket off her shoulders, my mouth barely leaving hers. I cannot get enough of how she tastes, I damn sure can't get enough of how she feels, and my hands are all over her, caressing her breasts, my finger ripping away a button of her silk blouse.

"You owe me a button and alterations," she hisses, tugging at the buttons of my vest. "And I hate this thing."

I walk her backward and press her against the desk. "And I hate these damn buttons," I say, yanking two more off.

"Reid!"

I snap the front clasp of her bra free.

Her hands go to my arms and I pant out, "I'll buy you another."

"What are we doing, Reid? We work together. You're my—"

"Boss," I supply, cupping her backside and molding her closer. "*Yes*. I am. Start remembering it."

"I remember, and hate that fact, quite well."

"Like you hate me?" I challenge.

"Right now?" she says. "Yes."

I tangle my fingers in her hair again, dragging her mouth to mine, "Exactly why we need to fuck," I say, cupping her breast and pinching her nipple. "So we can both stop thinking about how much we want to be naked together." I kiss her again, swallowing another of her soft, sexy moans while yanking her skirt up her hips, over the lace of her black thigh-highs to her hips.

With that sweet little ass of hers finally bare to my touch, I palm it and squeeze. She yanks hard on my tie, and I have no idea how that makes me hotter and harder, but it does. She does. Every taste of her. Every sound she makes. Everything she does. "Can you just be inside me already?" she demands.

I could, I think. I should want to, but that question, that need in her to just do this and be beyond it and me, grates down my spine in an unexpected way. I don't like it. I turn her and press her to the desk, forcing her to catch herself on the smooth surface. Her ass is perfect, and that too should please me, but it pisses me off. I smack her backside and she yelps, looking over her shoulder.

"Did you really just—"

I yank the red silk of her panties, and the tiny strings rip under my tug. She gasps, and I step into her, smacking her backside again. "Yes," I say, my hand sliding around her, fingers cupping her sex, my lips by her ear. "I did, and," I stroke through the slick wet heat of her sex, "you liked it."

"I didn't—"

I turn her, and kiss her, my tongue doing a quick, deep slide before I demand, "What happened to trust? I can't trust you if you lie to me."

"I don't lie," she says, yanking at my tie again. "Maybe you just think I lie because that's all you know."

"And yet, I never deny anything that feels good the way you just did." I lift her and set her on the desk, spreading her legs and settling on my knees in front of her.

She tries to squeeze her legs together but it's too late. My hands catch her knees, opening her wide. Her eyes meet mine. "You want to pay me back, don't you? That's what this is?"

"You mean lick you until you almost come and then cuff you to the chair and leave you? I could. You wouldn't even stop me." I drag one of her legs over my shoulder, her hips shifting forward, and I lick her clit. "But I'm not going to pay you back," I say, the taste of her on my lips rocketing through my senses. "I want you to come on my tongue again."

"I don't believe you," she whispers, swallowing hard. "I want—"

"Finally, you say it. You want. *I want.*" I lick her again, and she tilts her head back, moaning softly, and that easily she's giving me that submission I want from her. Pushing her to give me more, I suckle her, stroking two fingers along the seam of her sex and then sliding them inside her. She arches her hips, lifting into my mouth, into the pump of my fingers and I love this about her. She's not shy about wanting. She might resist, but once she commits, she's all the way.

"Oh God," she cries out, and then her body is tensing, only seconds before she spasms around my fingers, her legs quaking, and I do own her in this moment. Fuck. I want to own this woman more and that pisses me off. This is a fuck. This is one fuck. I don't ease her into completion. I strip away my fingers and mouth and while she gasps, I shrug out of my jacket, remove my wallet, yank out a condom, and stand up.

Her eyes meet mine with a punch between us that I tell myself is just how badly we both need me to be inside her. That it could be anything else is why I grip her hair, and not gently, reminding her of who is in control. "Now I taste like you again," I say, "but I never forgot how you taste." I close my mouth over hers, a wicked hot kiss, that equals an explosion of lust between us.

I'm kissing her. She's kissing me. My hands are all over her, but hers are on me, too. Stroking my cock through my pants, her fingers driving me crazy. At some point, I rip open the condom and she isn't shy. She's the one that unzips me. She's the one who pulls my erection free, her soft hands stroking along my ridiculously hard length. It's her who puts on the condom and me that cups her backside, pulls her to the edge of the desk and then, when I should just drive into her, fuck her finally, here and now, I tease us both. I stroke my cock along her sex until she hisses, "Enough already. Or not enough. Reid, damn it, I—"

My mouth comes down on hers, my tongue wanting to taste my name on her lips while I press my cock inside her and drive deep, burying myself to the hilt. Our lips part and our foreheads press together, and suddenly we're breathing together, not moving. Why the hell am I not moving? And yet, I'm not. I'm savoring rather than devouring, and that's not what this is. This is sex, hard, ready now sex, and I pull back and thrust into her. She moans, and I drive again, pressing her backward, forcing her to hold onto the desk behind her, not me. But I don't let that become an escape. I'm right here, I'm kissing her. I'm licking her nipple. I'm pumping into her, and yet, it's not enough. I slide my hand between her shoulder blades and lift her off of the desk, holding all of her weight. Somehow we're just there, melded close, and breathing together again, and then kissing again, our bodies more grinding than pumping us into that sweet spot of release.

Carrie gasps and stiffens again, and the minute she begins to orgasm I'm right there with her, my body clenching with the force of my release. I hold her tighter and at some point, I set her back on the desk, gripping it on one side while my other palm remains between her shoulder blades. My face is buried in her neck, and I come back to reality to the feel of her fingers flexing on my shoulders. I want to kiss her again and that is not normal for me. I should pull out. I should end this as fast and hard as we just fucked, and move on, but I don't. What the hell is this woman doing to me? I linger there with her, her body soft and yielding next to mine. I inhale the floral scent of her, and I know, I *know* that I am not done with this woman.

FIND OUT MORE ABOUT DIRTY RICH OBSESSION HERE:

https://dirtyrich.weebly.com/dirty-rich-obsession.html

EXCERPT FROM DIRTY RICH BETRAYAL

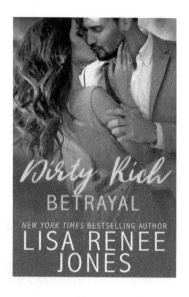

Mia

He kisses me, a quick brush of lips over lips. "I need you naked. I need to feel you next to me." He rolls me to my back and with that "for now" in the air, he moves and resettles with his lips to my stomach and this is not an accidental connection. My heart squeezes with the certainty that he's reminding me of how many times he told me he wanted a little girl just like me. It affects me. We had so many plans. We were best friends. We were so many things that happened so very quickly and easily, and then it was gone.

He pulls down my pants, and all too quickly my sneakers and everything else are gone. I'm naked and not just my body. I am so very naked with this man and always have been. But as for my body, I'm not alone for long. He strips away his clothes, and I lift to my elbows to admire all that sinewy, perfect muscle before he reaches down, grabs my legs and pulls me to him. The minute my backside is on the edge of the bed, he goes down on a knee. I sit up and cup his face. "Not now. Now I need—I need—"

He cups my head and pulls my mouth to his, kissing me with a long stroke of his tongue before he says, "And I need to taste you."

"Not now. I'm not leaving. We have time. I need—you. Here with me."

His eyes soften but he still leans in and licks my clit, and then suckles. I'm all but undone by the sensation because one thing I know and know well is how good this man is with his tongue. But he doesn't ignore my request. He pushes off the floor, and in a heartbeat, he's kissing me and I don't even know how we end up in the center of the bed, our naked bodies entwined. We just are and it's wonderful and right in ways nothing has been in so very long.

He lifts my leg to his thigh and presses his thick erection inside me, filling me in ways that go beyond our bodies; driving deep, his hand on my backside, pulling me into him, pushing into me, but then we don't move. Then we just lay there, intimately connected, lost in the moment and each other. "Is this what you wanted?"

"Yes," I say. "This is what I wanted."

"I didn't think I'd ever have you here, like this, with me again."

"Me either," I whisper, my fingers curling on his jaw. "Grayson," I say for no reason other than I need his name on my lips. I need everything with this man.

He kisses me, a fast, deep, passionate kiss. "I missed the hell out of you, Mia. So *fucking* much. I don't think you really understand how much."

This moment, right here, right now, is one of our raw, honest, perfect moments that has always made his betrayal hard to accept. I need that honesty in my life and with him and I don't even think about denying him my truth. "I missed you, too. More than you know, Grayson."

He squeezes my backside and drives into me again. I pant with the sensations that rip through my body, my hand going to his shoulder. "Nothing was right without you," he says. "Nothing, Mia." He kisses me, and I sink into the connection, pressing into him, into his thrust, into the

hard warmth of his entire body. Needing to be close.
Needing the things that separated us not to exist.

**FIND OUT MORE ABOUT DIRTY RICH
BETRAYAL HERE:**

**https://dirtyrich.weebly.com/dirty-rich-
betrayal.html**

ALSO BY LISA RENEE JONES

THE INSIDE OUT SERIES

If I Were You

Being Me

Revealing Us

His Secrets*

Rebecca's Lost Journals

The Master Undone*

My Hunger*

No In Between

My Control*

I Belong to You

All of Me*

THE SECRET LIFE OF AMY BENSEN

Escaping Reality

Infinite Possibilities

Forsaken

*Unbroken**

CARELESS WHISPERS

Denial

Demand

Surrender

WHITE LIES

Provocative

Shameless

TALL, DARK & DEADLY

Hot Secrets

Dangerous Secrets

Beneath the Secrets

WALKER SECURITY

Deep Under

Pulled Under

Falling Under

LILAH LOVE

Murder Notes
Murder Girl

DIRTY RICH

Dirty Rich One Night Stand
Dirty Rich Cinderella Story
Dirty Rich Obsession
Dirty Rich Betrayal
Dirty Rich Cinderella Story: Ever After
Dirty Rich One Night Stand: Two Years Later (Dec. 2018)
Dirty Rich Obsession: All Mine (Jan. 2019)

THE FILTHY DUET

The Bastard (Nov. 2018)
The Princess (Jan. 2018)

*eBook only

ABOUT THE AUTHOR

New York Times and USA Today bestselling author Lisa Renee Jones is the author of the highly acclaimed INSIDE OUT series.

In addition to the success of Lisa's INSIDE OUT series, she has published many successful titles. The TALL, DARK AND DEADLY series and THE SECRET LIFE OF AMY BENSEN series, both spent several months on a combination of the New York Times and USA Today bestselling lists. Lisa is also the author of the bestselling the bestselling DIRTY MONEY and WHITE LIES series. And will be publishing the first book in her Lilah Love suspense series with Amazon Publishing in March 2018.

Prior to publishing Lisa owned multi-state staffing agency that was recognized many times by The Austin Business Journal and also praised by the Dallas Women's Magazine. In 1998 Lisa was listed as the #7 growing women owned business in Entrepreneur Magazine.

Lisa loves to hear from her readers. You can reach her at www.lisareneejones.com and she is active on Twitter and Facebook daily.

CPSIA information can be obtained
at www.ICGtesting.com
Printed in the USA
LVHW09s1811171018
593930LV00001B/85/P

9 781726 804837